Emily J. Harding, Alex. Chodsko

Fairy Tales of the Slav Peasants and Herdsmen

Emily J. Harding, Alex. Chodsko

Fairy Tales of the Slav Peasants and Herdsmen

ISBN/EAN: 9783337071028

Printed in Europe, USA, Canada, Australia, Japan

Cover: Foto ©Andreas Hilbeck / pixelio.de

More available books at **www.hansebooks.com**

SLAV TALES

GEORGE ALLEN
156 CHARING CROSS ROAD
PUBLISHER LONDON
RUSKIN HOUSE

From "*The Plentiful Tablecloth*," *p.* 351.

Fairy Tales of the * * *
Slav Peasants and
Herdsmen From the
French of Alex. Chodsko
Translated and Illustrated
by Emily J. Harding

London: George Allen
156 Charing Cross Road
1896

NOTE BY THE PUBLISHER

VERY few of the twenty fairy tales included in this volume have been presented before in an English dress; this will doubtless enhance their value in the eyes of the young folk, for whom, principally, they are intended. It is hoped that older readers will find some additional interest in tracing throughout the many evidences of kinship between these stories and those of more pronounced Eastern origin.

The translation has been carefully revised by a well-known writer, who has interfered as little as possible with the original text, except in those instances where slight alterations were necessary.

The illustrations speak for themselves, and are what might have been expected from the artist who designed those for the "Lullabies of Many Lands," issued last Christmas.

November 1895.

CONTENTS.

x   CONTENTS

LIST OF ILLUSTRATIONS

THE ABODE OF THE GODS

A

The Two Brothers

ONCE upon a time there were two brothers whose father had left them but a small fortune. The eldest grew very rich, but at the same time cruel and wicked, whereas there was nowhere a more honest or kinder man than the younger. But he remained poor, and had many children, so that at times they could scarcely get bread to eat. At last, one day there was not even this in the house, so he went to his rich brother and asked him for a loaf of bread. Waste of time! His rich brother only called him beggar and vagabond, and slammed the door in his face.

The poor fellow, after this brutal reception, did not know which way to turn. Hungry, scantily clad, shivering with cold, his legs could scarcely carry him along. He had not the heart to go home, with nothing for the children, so he went towards the mountain forest. But all he found there were some wild pears that had fallen to the ground. He had to content himself with eating these, though they set his teeth on edge. But what was he to do to warm himself, for the east wind with its chill blast pierced him through and through. "Where shall I go?" he said; "what will become of us in the cottage? There is neither food nor fire, and my brother has driven me from his door." It was just then he remembered having heard that the top of the mountain in front of him was made of crystal, and had a fire for ever burning upon it. "I will try and find it," he said, "and then I may be able to warm myself a little." So he went on climbing higher and higher till he reached the top, when he was startled to see twelve strange beings sitting round a huge fire. He stopped for a moment, but then said to himself, "What have I to lose? Why should I fear? God is with me. Courage!"

So he advanced towards the fire, and bowing respectfully, said: "Good people, take pity on my distress. I am very poor, no one cares for me, I have not even a fire in my cottage; will you let me warm myself at yours?" They all looked kindly at him, and one of them said: "My son, come sit down with us and warm yourself."

So he sat down, and felt warm directly he was near them. But he dared not speak while they were silent. What astonished him most was that they changed seats one after another, and in such a way that each one passed round the fire and came back to his own place. When he drew near the fire an old man with long white beard and bald head arose from the flames and spoke to him thus:

"Man, waste not thy life here; return to thy cottage, work, and live honestly. Take as many embers as thou wilt, we have more than we need."

And having said this he disappeared. Then the twelve filled a large sack with embers, and, putting it on the poor man's shoulders, advised him to hasten home.

Humbly thanking them, he set off. As he went he wondered why the embers did not feel hot, and why they should weigh no more than a sack of paper. He was thankful that he should be able to have a fire, but imagine his astonishment when on arriving home he found the sack to contain as many gold pieces as there had been embers; he almost went out of his mind with joy at the possession of so much money. With all his heart he thanked those who had been so ready to help him in his need.

He was now rich, and rejoiced to be able to provide for his family. Being curious to find out how many gold pieces there were, and not knowing how to count, he sent his wife to his rich brother for the loan of a quart measure.

This time the brother was in a better temper, so he lent what was asked of him, but said mockingly, "What can such beggars as you have to measure?"

The wife replied, "Our neighbour owes us some wheat; we want to be sure he returns us the right quantity."

The rich brother was puzzled, and suspecting something he, unknown to his sister-in-law, put some grease inside the measure. The trick succeeded, for on getting it back he found a piece of gold sticking to it. Filled with astonishment, he could only suppose his brother had joined a band of robbers: so he hurried to his brother's cottage, and threatened to bring him before the Justice of the Peace if he did not confess where the gold came from. The poor man was troubled, and, dreading to offend his brother, told the story of his journey to the Crystal Mountain.

Now the elder brother had plenty of money for himself, yet he was envious of the brother's good fortune, and became greatly displeased when he found that his brother won every one's esteem by the good use he made of his wealth. At last he determined to visit the Crystal Mountain himself.

"I may meet with as good luck as my brother," said he to himself.

Upon reaching the Crystal Mountain he found the twelve seated round the fire as before, and thus addressed them:

"I beg of you, good people, to let me warm myself, for it is bitterly cold, and I am poor and homeless."

But one of them replied, "My son, the hour of thy birth was favourable; thou art rich, but a miser; thou art wicked, for thou hast dared to lie to us. Well dost thou deserve thy punishment."

Amazed and terrified he stood silent, not daring to speak. Meanwhile the twelve changed places one after another, each at last returning to his own seat. Then from the midst of the flames arose the white-bearded old man and spoke thus sternly to the rich man:

"Woe unto the wilful! Thy brother is virtuous, therefore have I blessed him. As for thee, thou art wicked, and so shalt not escape our vengeance."

At these words the twelve arose. The first seized the unfortunate man, struck him, and passed him on to the second; the second also struck him and passed him on to the third; and so did they all in their turn, until he was given up to the old man, who disappeared with him into the fire.

Days, weeks, months went by, but the rich man never returned, and none knew what had become of him. I think, between you and me, the younger brother had his suspicions but he very wisely kept them to himself.

II

TIME AND THE KINGS OF THE ELEMENTS

THERE was once a married pair who loved each other tenderly. The husband would not have given up his wife for all the riches in the world, while her first thought was how best to please him. So they were very happy, and lived like two grains in one ear of corn.

One day while working in the fields, a great longing came over him to see her: so without waiting for the hour of sunset he ran home. Alas! she was not there. He looked high and low, he ran here, there, and everywhere, he wept, he called to her; in vain! his dear wife was not to be found.

So heartbroken was he that he no longer cared to live. He could think of nothing but the loss of his dear wife and how to find her again. At last he determined to travel all over the world in search of her. So he began to walk straight on, trusting God to direct his steps. Sad and thoughtful, he wandered for many days, until he reached a cottage close by the shores of a large lake. Here he stopped, hoping to find out news. On entering the cottage he was met by a woman, who tried to prevent him entering.

"What do you want here, unlucky wretch?" said she. "If my husband sees you, he will kill you instantly."

"Who is your husband then?" asked the traveller.

"What! you do not know him? My husband is the Water-King; everything under water obeys him. Depart quickly, for if he finds you here he will certainly devour you."

"Perhaps after all he would take pity on me. But hide me somewhere, for I am worn and weary, and without shelter for the night."

So the Water-Queen was persuaded, and hid him behind the stove. Almost immediately after the Water-King entered. He had barely crossed the threshold when he called out, "Wife, I smell human flesh; give it me quickly, for I am hungry." She dared not disobey him, and so she had to tell him of the traveller's hiding-place. The poor man became terribly frightened, and trembled in every limb, and began to stammer out excuses.

"I assure you I have done no harm. I came here in search of news of my poor wife. Oh, do help me to find her; I cannot live without her."

"Well," replied the Water-King, "as you love your wife so tenderly I will forgive you for coming here, but I cannot help you to find her, for I do not know where she is. Yet I remember seeing two ducks on the lake yesterday, perchance she is one of them. But I should advise you to ask my brother the Fire-King; he may be able to tell you more."

Happy to have escaped so easily, he thanked the Water-King and set out to find the Fire-King. But the latter was unable to help him, and could only advise him to consult his other brother, the Air-King. But the Air-King, though he had travelled all over the earth, could only say he thought he had seen a woman at the foot of the Crystal Mountain.

But the traveller was cheered at the news, and went to seek his wife at the foot of the Crystal Mountain, which was close to their cottage. On reaching it he began at once to climb the mountain by making his way up the bed of the torrent that came rushing down there. Several ducks that were in the pools near the waterfall called out, "My good man, don't go up there; you'll be killed."

But he walked fearlessly on till he came to some thatched cottages, at the largest of which he stopped. Here a crowd of wizards and witches surrounded him, screaming at the top of their voices, "What are you looking for?"

"My wife," said he.

"She is here," they cried, "but you cannot take her away unless you recognise her among two hundred women all exactly like her."

"What! Not know my own wife? Why, here she is,"

said he, as he clasped her in his arms. And she, delighted to be with him again, kissed him fondly. Then she whispered:

"Dearest, though you knew me to-day I doubt whether you will to-morrow, for there will be so many of us all alike. Now I will tell you what to do. At nightfall go to the top of the Crystal Mountain, where live the King of Time and his court. Ask him how you may know me. If you are good and honest he will help you; if not, he will devour you whole at one mouthful."

"I will do what you advise, dear one," he replied, "but tell me, why did you leave me so suddenly? If you only knew what I have suffered! I have sought you all over the world."

"I did not leave you willingly," said she. "A country-man asked me to come and look at the mountain torrent. When we got there he sprinkled some water over himself, and at once I saw wings growing out of his shoulders, and he soon changed his shape entirely into that of a drake; and I too became a duck at the same time, and whether I would or no I was obliged to follow him. Here I was allowed to resume my own form; and now there is but the one difficulty of being recognised by you."

So they parted, she to join the other women, he to continue his way to the Crystal Mountain. At the top he found twelve strange beings sitting round a large fire: they were the attendants of the King of Time. He saluted them respectfully.

"What dost thou want?" said they.

"I have lost my dear wife. Can you tell me how to

recognise her among two hundred other women all exactly alike?"

"No," said they, "but perhaps our King can."

Then arose from the midst of the flames an old man with bald head and long white beard, who, on hearing his request, replied: "Though all these women be exactly alike, thy wife will have a black thread in the shoe of her right foot."

So saying he vanished, and the traveller, thanking the twelve, descended the mountain.

Sure it is that without the black thread he would never have recognised her. And though the Magician tried to hide her, the spell was broken; and the two returned rejoicing to their home, where they lived happily ever after.

III

THE TWELVE MONTHS

THERE was once a widow who had two daughters, Helen,
her own child by her dead husband, and Marouckla,
his daughter by his first wife. She loved Helen, but hated

the poor orphan, because she was far prettier than her own daughter. Marouckla did not think about her good looks, and could not understand why her stepmother should be angry at the sight of her. The hardest work fell to her share; she cleaned out the rooms, cooked, washed, sewed, spun, wove, brought in the hay, milked the cow, and all this without any help. Helen, meanwhile, did nothing but dress herself in her best clothes and go to one amusement after another. But Marouckla never complained; she bore the scoldings and bad temper of mother and sister with a smile on her lips, and the patience of a lamb. But this angelic behaviour did not soften them. They became even more tyrannical and grumpy, for Marouckla grew daily more beautiful, while Helen's ugliness increased. So the stepmother determined to get rid of Marouckla, for she knew that while she remained her own daughter would have no suitors. Hunger, every kind of privation, abuse, every means was used to make the girl's life miserable. The most wicked of men could not have been more mercilessly cruel than these two vixens. But in spite of it all Marouckla grew ever sweeter and more charming.

One day in the middle of winter Helen wanted some wood-violets.

"Listen," cried she to Marouckla; "you must go up the mountain and find me some violets, I want some to put in my gown; they must be fresh and sweet-scented—do you hear?"

"But, my dear sister, who ever heard of violets blooming in the snow?" said the poor orphan.

"You wretched creature! Do you dare to disobey me?"

said Helen. "Not another word; off with you. If you do not bring me some violets from the mountain forest, I will kill you."

The stepmother also added her threats to those of Helen, and with vigorous blows they pushed Marouckla outside and shut the door upon her. The weeping girl made her way to the mountain. The snow lay deep, and there was no trace of any human being. Long she wandered hither and thither, and lost herself in the wood. She was hungry, and shivered with cold, and prayed to die. Suddenly she saw a light in the distance, and climbed towards it, till she reached the top of the mountain. Upon the highest peak burnt a large fire, surrounded by twelve blocks of stone, on which sat twelve strange beings. Of these the first three had white hair, three were not quite so old, three were young and handsome, and the rest still younger.

There they all sate silently looking at the fire. They were the twelve months of the year. The great Setchène (January) was placed higher than the others; his hair and moustache were white as snow, and in his hand he held a wand. At first Marouckla was afraid, but after a while her courage returned, and drawing near she said:

"Men of God, may I warm myself at your fire? I am chilled by the winter cold."

The great Setchène raised his head and answered:

"What brings thee here, my daughter? What dost thou seek?"

"I am looking for violets," replied the maiden.

"This is not the season for violets; dost thou not see the snow everywhere?" said Setchène.

"I know well, but my sister Helen and my stepmother have ordered me to bring them violets from your mountain: if I return without them they will kill me. I pray you, good shepherds, tell me where they may be found?"

Here the great Setchène arose and went over to the youngest of the months, and placing his wand in his hand, said:

"Brother Brezène (March), do thou take the highest place."

Brezène obeyed, at the same time waving his wand over the fire. Immediately the flames rose towards the sky, the snow began to melt and the trees and shrubs to bud; the grass became green, and from between its blades peeped the pale primrose. It was Spring, and the meadows were blue with violets.

"Gather them quickly, Marouckla," said Brezène.

Joyfully she hastened to pick the flowers, and having soon a large bunch she thanked them and ran home. Helen and the stepmother were amazed at the sight of the flowers, the scent of which filled the house.

"Where did you find them?" asked Helen.

"Under the trees on the mountain slope," said Marouckla.

Helen kept the flowers for herself and her mother; she did not even thank her step-sister for the trouble she had taken. The next day she desired Marouckla to fetch her strawberries.

"Run," said she, "and fetch me strawberries from the mountain: they must be very sweet and ripe."

"But who ever heard of strawberries ripening in the snow?" exclaimed Marouckla.

"Hold your tongue, worm; don't answer me; if I don't have my strawberries I will kill you."

Then the stepmother pushed her into the yard and bolted the door. The unhappy girl made her way towards the mountain and to the large fire round which sat the twelve months. The great Setchène occupied the highest place.

"Men of God, may I warm myself at your fire? The winter cold chills me," said she, drawing near.

The great Setchène raised his head and asked:

"Why comest thou here? What dost thou seek?"

"I am looking for strawberries," said she.

"We are in the midst of winter," replied Setchène; "strawberries do not grow in the snow."

"I know," said the girl sadly, "but my sister and stepmother have ordered me to bring them strawberries; if I do not they will kill me. Pray, good shepherds, tell me where to find them."

The great Setchène arose, crossed over to the month opposite him, and putting the wand into his hand, said:

"Brother Tchervène (June), do thou take the highest place."

Tchervène obeyed, and as he waved his wand over the fire the flames leapt towards the sky. Instantly the snow melted, the earth was covered with verdure, trees were clothed with leaves, birds began to sing, and various flowers blossomed in the forest. It was summer. Under the bushes masses of star-shaped flowers changed into ripening strawberries. Before Marouckla had time to cross herself they covered the glade, making it look like a sea of blood.

"Gather them quickly, Marouckla," said Tchervène.

Joyfully she thanked the months, and having filled her apron ran happily home. Helen and her mother wondered at seeing the strawberries, which filled the house with their delicious fragrance.

"Wherever did you find them?" asked Helen crossly.

"Right up among the mountains; those from under the beech trees are not bad."

Helen gave a few to her mother and ate the rest herself; not one did she offer to her step-sister. Being tired of strawberries, on the third day she took a fancy for some fresh red apples.

"Run, Marouckla," said she, "and fetch me fresh red apples from the mountain."

"Apples in winter, sister? why, the trees have neither leaves nor fruit."

"Idle slut, go this minute," said Helen; "unless you bring back apples we will kill you."

As before, the stepmother seized her roughly and turned her out of the house. The poor girl went weeping up the mountain, across the deep snow upon which lay no human footprint, and on towards the fire round which were the twelve months. Motionless sat they, and on the highest stone was the great Setchène.

"Men of God, may I warm myself at your fire? The winter cold chills me," said she, drawing near.

The great Setchène raised his head.

"Why com'st thou here? What dost thou seek?" asked he.

"I am come to look for red apples," replied Marouckla.

"But this is winter, and not the season for red apples," observed the great Setchène.

"I know," answered the girl, "but my sister and stepmother sent me to fetch red apples from the mountain; if I return without them they will kill me."

Thereupon the great Setchène arose and went over to one of the elderly months, to whom he handed the wand, saying:

"Brother Zaré (September), do thou take the highest place."

Zaré moved to the highest stone and waved his wand over the fire. There was a flare of red flames, the snow disappeared, but the fading leaves which trembled on the trees were sent by a cold north-east wind in yellow masses to the glade. Only a few flowers of autumn were visible, such as the fleabane and red gillyflower, autumn colchicums in the ravine, and under the beeches bracken and tufts of northern heather. At first Marouckla looked in vain for red apples. Then she espied a tree which grew at a great height, and from the branches of this hung the bright red fruit. Zaré ordered her to gather some quickly. The girl was delighted and shook the tree. First one apple fell, then another.

"That is enough," said Zaré, "hurry home."

Thanking the months, she returned joyfully. Helen marvelled and the stepmother wondered at seeing the fruit.

"Where did you gather them?" asked the step-sister.

"There are more on the mountain top," answered Marouckla.

"Then why did you not bring more?" said Helen angrily; "you must have eaten them on your way back, you wicked girl."

"No, dear sister, I have not even tasted them," said Marouckla. "I shook the tree twice; one apple fell each time. I was not allowed to shake it again, but was told to return home."

"May Perun smite you with his thunderbolt," said Helen, striking her.

Marouckla prayed to die rather than suffer such ill-treatment. Weeping bitterly, she took refuge in the kitchen. Helen and her mother found the apples more delicious than any they had ever tasted, and when they had eaten both longed for more.

"Listen, mother," said Helen. "Give me my cloak; I will fetch some more apples myself, or else that good-for-nothing wretch will eat them all on the way. I shall be able to find the mountain and the tree. The shepherds may cry 'Stop,' but I shall not leave go till I have shaken down all the apples."

In spite of her mother's advice she put on her pelisse, covered her head with a warm hood, and took the road to the mountain. The mother stood and watched her till she was lost in the distance.

Snow covered everything, not a human footprint was to be seen on its surface. Helen lost herself and wandered hither and thither. After a while she saw a light above her, and following in its direction reached the mountain top. There was the flaming fire, the twelve blocks of stone, and the twelve months. At first she was frightened and hesitated; then she came nearer and warmed her hands. She did not ask permission, nor did she speak one polite word.

"What has brought thee here? What dost thou seek?" said the great Setchène severely.

"I am not obliged to tell you, old greybeard; what business

is it of yours?" she replied disdainfully, turning her back on the fire and going towards the forest.

The great Setchène frowned, and waved his wand over his head. Instantly the sky became covered with clouds, the fire went down, snow fell in large flakes, an icy wind howled round the mountain. Amid the fury of the storm Helen added curses against her step-sister. The pelisse failed to warm her benumbed limbs. The mother kept on waiting for her; she looked from the window, she watched from the doorstep, but her daughter came not. The hours passed slowly, but Helen did not return.

"Can it be that the apples have charmed her from her home?" thought the mother. Then she clad herself in hood and pelisse and went in search of her daughter. Snow fell in huge masses; it covered all things, it lay untouched by human footsteps. For long she wandered hither and thither; the icy north-east wind whistled in the mountain, but no voice answered her cries.

Day after day Marouckla worked and prayed, and waited; but neither stepmother nor sister returned, they had been frozen to death on the mountain. The inheritance of a small house, a field, and a cow fell to Marouckla. In course of time an honest farmer came to share them with her, and their lives were happy and peaceful.

THE SUN

OR

THE THREE GOLDEN HAIRS OF THE OLD MAN VSÉVÈDE

THE SUN; OR, THE THREE GOLDEN HAIRS
OF THE OLD MAN VSÉVÈDE

CAN this be a true story? It is said that once there was a king who was exceedingly fond of hunting the wild beasts in his forests. One day he followed a stag so far and so long that he lost his way. Alone and overtaken by night, he was glad to find himself near a small thatched cottage in which lived a charcoal-burner.

“Will you kindly show me the way to the high-road? You shall be handsomely rewarded.”

“I would willingly,” said the charcoal-burner, “but God is going to send my wife a little child, and I cannot leave her alone. Will you pass the night under our roof? There is a truss of sweet hay in the loft where you may rest, and to-morrow morning I will be your guide.”

The king accepted the invitation and went to bed in the loft. Shortly after a son was born to the charcoal-burner’s wife. But the king could not sleep. At midnight he heard noises in the house, and looking through a crack in the flooring he saw the charcoal-burner asleep, his wife almost in a faint, and by the side of the newly-born babe three old women dressed in white, each holding a lighted taper in her hand, and all talking together. Now these were the three Soudiché or Fates, you must know.

The first said, “On this boy I bestow the gift of confronting great dangers.”

The second said, “I bestow the power of happily escaping all these dangers, and of living to a good old age.”

The third said, “I bestow upon him for wife the princess born at the selfsame hour as he, and daughter of the very king sleeping above in the loft.”

At these words the lights went out and silence reigned around.

Now the king was greatly troubled, and wondered exceedingly; he felt as if he had received a sword-thrust in the chest. He lay awake all night thinking how to prevent the words of the Fates from coming true.

With the first glimmer of morning light the baby began

to cry. The charcoal-burner, on going over to it, found that his wife was dead.

"Poor little orphan," he said sadly, "what will become of thee without a mother's care?"

"Confide this child to me," said the king, "I will look after it. He shall be well provided for. You shall be given a sum of money large enough to keep you without having to burn charcoal."

The poor man gladly agreed, and the king went away promising to send some one for the child. The queen and courtiers thought it would be an agreeable surprise for the king to hear that a charming little princess had been born on the night he was away. But instead of being pleased he frowned, and calling one of his servants, said to him, "Go to the charcoal-burner's cottage in the forest, and give the man this purse in exchange for a new-born infant. On your way back drown the child. See well that he is drowned, for if he should in any way escape, you yourself shall suffer in his place."

The servant was given the child in a basket, and on reaching the centre of a narrow bridge that stretched across a wide and deep river, he threw both basket and baby into the water.

"A prosperous journey to you, Mr. Son-in-Law," said the king, on hearing the servant's story: for he fully believed the child was drowned. But it was far from being the case; the little one was floating happily along in its basket cradle, and slumbering as sweetly as if his mother had sung him to sleep. Now it happened that a fisherman, who was mending his nets before his cottage door, saw the basket floating down the river. He jumped at once into his boat, picked it up, and ran to tell his wife the good news.

"Look," said he, "you have always longed for a son; here is a beautiful little boy the river has sent us."

The woman was delighted, and took the infant and loved it as her own child. They named him *Plavacek* (the floater), because he had come to them floating on the water.

The river flowed on. Years passed away. The little baby grew into a handsome youth; in all the villages round there were none to compare with him. Now it happened that one summer day the king was riding unattended. And the heat being very great he reined in his horse before the fisherman's door to ask for a drink of water. Plavacek brought the water. The king looked at him attentively, then turning to the fisherman, said, "That is a good-looking lad; is he your son?"

"He is and he isn't," replied the fisherman. "I found him, when he was quite a tiny baby, floating down the stream in a basket. So we adopted him and brought him up as our own son."

The king turned as pale as death, for he guessed that he was the same child he had ordered to be drowned. Then recovering himself he got down from his horse and said : "I want a trusty messenger to take a letter to the palace, could you send him with it?"

"With pleasure! Your majesty may be sure of its safe delivery."

Thereupon the king wrote to the queen as follows—

"The man who brings you this letter is the most dangerous of all my enemies. Have his head cut off at once;

no delay, no pity, he must be executed before my return. Such is my will and pleasure."

This he carefully folded and sealed with the royal seal.

Plavacek took the letter and set off immediately. But the forest through which he had to pass was so large, and the trees so thick, that he missed the path and was overtaken by the darkness before the journey was nearly over. In the midst of his trouble he met an old woman who said, "Where are you going, Plavacek? Where are you going?"

"I am the bearer of a letter from the king to the queen, but have missed the path to the palace. Could you, good mother, put me on the right road?"

"Impossible to-day, my child; it is getting dark, and you would not have time to get there. Stay with me to-night. You will not be with strangers, for I am your godmother."

Plavacek agreed. Thereupon they entered a pretty little cottage that seemed suddenly to sink into the earth. Now while he slept the old woman changed his letter for another, which ran thus:—

"Immediately upon the receipt of this letter introduce the bearer to the princess our daughter. I have chosen this young man for my son-in-law, and it is my wish they should be married before my return to the palace. Such is my pleasure."

The letter was duly delivered, and when the queen had read it, she ordered everything to be prepared for the wedding. Both she and her daughter greatly enjoyed Plavacek's society, and nothing disturbed the happiness of the newly married pair.

Within a few days the king returned, and on hearing what had taken place was very angry with the queen.

"But you expressly bade me have the wedding before your return. Come, read your letter again, here it is," said she.

He closely examined the letter; the paper, handwriting, seal—all were undoubtedly his. He then called his son-in-law, and questioned him about his journey. Plavacek hid nothing: he told how he had lost his way, and how he had passed the night in a cottage in the forest.

"What was the old woman like?" asked the king.

From Plavacek's description the king knew it was the very same who, twenty years before, had foretold the marriage of the princess with the charcoal-burner's son. After some moments' thought the king said, "What is done is done. But you will not become my son-in-law so easily. No, i' faith! As a wedding present you must bring me three golden hairs from the head of Dède-Vsévède."

In this way he thought to get rid of his son-in-law, whose very presence was distasteful to him. The young fellow took leave of his wife and set off. "I know not which way to go," said he to himself, "but my godmother the witch will surely help me."

But he found the way easily enough. He walked on and on and on for a long time over mountain, valley, and river, until he reached the shores of the Black Sea. There he found a boat and boatman.

"May God bless you, old boatman," said he.

"And you, too, my young traveller. Where are you going?"

"To Dède-Vsévède's castle for three of his golden hairs."

"Ah, then you are very welcome. For a long weary while I have been waiting for such a messenger as you. I have been ferrying passengers across for these twenty years, and not one of them has done anything to help me. If you will promise to ask Dède-Vsévède when I shall be released from my toil I will row you across."

Plavacek promised, and was rowed to the opposite bank. He continued his journey on foot until he came in sight of a large town half in ruins, near which was passing a funeral procession. The king of that country was following his father's coffin, and with the tears running down his cheeks.

" May God comfort you in your distress," said Plavacek.

"Thank you, good traveller. Where are you going?"

"To the house of Dède-Vsévède in quest of three of his golden hairs."

"To the house of Dède-Vsévède? indeed! What a pity you did not come sooner, we have long been expecting such a messenger as you. Come and see me by and bye."

When Plavacek presented himself at court the king said to him:

"We understand you are on your way to the house of Dède-Vsévède? Now we have an apple-tree here that bears the fruit of everlasting youth. One of these apples eaten by a man, even though he be dying, will cure him and make him young again. For the last twenty years neither fruit nor flower has been found on this tree. Will you ask Dède-Vsévède the cause of it?"

"That I will, with pleasure."

Then Plavacek continued his journey, and as he went he came to a large and beautiful city where all was sad and silent. Near the gate was an old man who leant on a stick and walked with difficulty.

"May God bless you, good old man."

"And you, too, my handsome young traveller. Where are you going?"

"To Dède-Vsévède's palace in search of three of his golden hairs."

"Ah, you are the very messenger I have so long waited for. Allow me to take you to my master the king."

On their arrival at the palace, the king said, "I hear you are an ambassador to Dède-Vsévède. We have here a well, the water of which renews itself. So wonderful are its effects that invalids are immediately cured on drinking it, while a few drops sprinkled on a corpse will bring it to life again. For the past twenty years this well has remained dry: if you will ask old Dède-Vsévède how the flow of water may be restored I will reward you royally."

Plavacek promised to do so, and was dismissed with good wishes. He then travelled through deep dark forests, in the midst of which might be seen a large meadow; out of it grew lovely flowers, and in the centre stood a castle built of gold. It was the home of Dède-Vsévède. So brilliant with light was it that it seemed to be built of fire. When he entered there was no one there but an old woman spinning.

"Greeting, Plavacek, I am well pleased to see you."

She was his godmother, who had given him shelter in her cottage when he was the bearer of the king's letter.

"Tell me what brings you here from such a distance," she went on.

"The king would not have me for his son-in-law, unless I first got him three golden hairs from the head of Dède-Vsévède. So he sent me here to fetch them."

The Fate laughed. "Dède-Vsévède indeed! Why, I am his mother, it is the shining sun himself. He is a child at morning time, a grown man at midday, a decrepit old man, looking as if he had lived a hundred years, at eventide. But I will see that you have the three hairs from his head; I am not your godmother for nothing. All the same you must not remain here. My son is a good lad, but when he comes home he is hungry, and would very probably order you to be roasted for his supper. Now I will turn this empty bucket upside down, and you shall hide underneath it."

Plavacek begged the Fate to obtain from Dède-Vsévède the answers to the three questions he had been asked.

"I will do so certainly, but you must listen to what he says."

Suddenly a blast of wind howled round the palace, and the Sun entered by a western window. He was an old man with golden hair.

"I smell human flesh," cried he, "I am sure of it. Mother, you have some one here."

"Star of day," she replied, "whom could I have here that you would not see sooner than I? The fact is that in your daily journeys the scent of human flesh is always with you, so when you come home at evening it clings to you still."

The old man said nothing, and sat down to supper. When he had finished he laid his golden head on the Fate's lap and went to sleep. Then she pulled out a hair and threw it on the ground. It fell with a metallic sound like the vibration of a guitar string.

"What do you want, mother?" asked he.

"Nothing, my son; I was sleeping, and had a strange dream."

"What was it, mother?"

"I thought I was in a place where there was a well, and the well was fed from a spring, the water of which cured all diseases. Even the dying were restored to health on drinking that water, and the dead who were sprinkled with it came to life again. For the last twenty years the well has run dry. What must be done to restore the flow of water?"

"That is very simple. A frog has lodged itself in the opening of the spring, this prevents the flow of water. Kill the frog, and the water will return to the well."

He slept again, and the old woman pulled out another golden hair, and threw it on the ground.

"Mother, what do you want?"

"Nothing, my son, nothing; I was dreaming. In my dream I saw a large town, the name of which I have forgotten. And there grew an apple-tree the fruit of which had the power to make the old young again. A single apple eaten by an old man would restore to him the vigour and freshness of youth. For twenty years this tree has not borne fruit. What can be done to make it fruitful?"

"The means are not difficult. A snake hidden among the roots destroys the sap. Kill the snake, transplant the tree, and the fruit will grow as before."

He again fell asleep, and the old woman pulled out another golden hair.

"Now look here, mother, why will you not let me sleep?" said the old man, really vexed; and he would have got up.

"Lie down, my darling son, do not disturb yourself. I am sorry I awoke you, but I have had a very strange dream. It seemed that I saw a boatman on the shores of the Black Sea, and he complained that he had been toiling at the ferry for twenty years without any one having come to take his place. For how much longer must this poor old man continue to row?"

"He is a silly fellow. He has but to place his oars in the hands of the first comer and jump ashore. Whoever receives the oars will replace him as ferryman. But leave me in peace now, mother, and do not wake me again. I have to rise very early, and must first dry the eyes of a princess. The poor thing spends all night weeping for her husband who has been sent by the king to get three of my golden hairs."

Next morning the wind whistled round Dède-Vsévède's palace, and instead of an old man, a beautiful child with golden hair awoke on the old woman's lap. It was the glorious sun. He bade her good-bye, and flew out of the eastern window. The old woman turned up the bucket and said to Plavacek, "Look, here are the three golden hairs. You now know the answers to your questions. May God direct you and send you a prosperous journey. You will not see me again, for you will have no further need of me."

He thanked her gratefully and left her. On arriving at the town with the dried-up well, he was questioned by the king as to what news he had brought.

"Have the well carefully cleaned out," said he, "kill the frog that obstructs the spring, and the wonderful water will flow again."

The king did as he was advised, and rejoiced to see the water return. He gave Plavacek twelve swan-white horses, and as much gold and silver as they could carry.

On reaching the second town and being asked by the king what news he had brought, he replied, "Excellent; one could not wish for better. Dig up your apple-tree, kill the snake that lies among the roots, transplant the tree, and it will produce apples like those of former times."

And all turned out as he had said, for no sooner was the tree replanted than it was covered with blossoms that gave it the appearance of a sea of roses. The delighted king gave him twelve raven-black horses, laden with as much wealth as they could carry. He then journeyed to the shores of the Black Sea. There the boatman questioned him as to what news he had brought respecting his release. Plavacek first crossed with his twenty-four horses to the opposite bank, and then replied that the boatman might gain his freedom by placing the oars in the hands of the first traveller who wished to be ferried over.

Plavacek's royal father-in-law could not believe his eyes when he saw Dède-Vsévède's three golden hairs. As for the princess, his young wife, she wept tears, but of joy, not sadness, to see her dear one again, and she said to him, "How did you get such splendid horses and so much wealth, dear husband?"

And he answered her, "All this represents the price paid for the weariness of spirit I have felt; it is the ready money for hardships endured and services given. Thus, I showed one king how to regain possession of the Apples of Youth: to another I told the secret of reopening the spring of water that gives health and life."

"Apples of Youth! Water of Life!" interrupted the king. "I will certainly go and find these treasures for myself. Ah, what joy! having eaten of these apples I shall become young again; having drunk of the Water of Immortality, I shall live for ever."

And he started off in search of these treasures. But he has not yet returned from his search.

KOVLAD

I

THE SOVEREIGN OF THE MINERAL KINGDOM

ONCE upon a time, and a long long time ago it was, there lived a widow who had a very pretty daughter. The mother, good honest woman, was quite content with her station in life. But with the daughter it was otherwise; she, like a spoilt beauty, looked contemptuously upon her many admirers, her mind was full of proud and ambitious thoughts, and the more lovers she had, the prouder she became.

One beautiful moonlight night the mother awoke, and being unable to sleep, began to pray God for the happiness of her only child, though she often made her mother's life miserable. The fond woman looked lovingly at the beautiful daughter sleeping by her side, and she wondered, as she saw her smile, what happy dream had visited her. Then she finished her prayer, and laying her head on the girl's pillow, fell asleep. Next day she said, "Come, darling child, tell me what you were dreaming about last night, you looked so happy smiling in your sleep."

"Oh yes, mother, I remember. I had a very beautiful dream. I thought a rich nobleman came to our house, in a splendid carriage of brass, and gave me a ring set with stones, that sparkled like the stars of heaven. When I entered the church with him, it was full of people, and they all thought me divine and adorable, like the Blessed Virgin."

"Ah! my child, what sin! May God keep you from such dreams."

But the daughter ran away singing, and busied herself about the house. The same day a handsome young farmer drove into the village in his cart and begged them to come and share his country bread. He was a kind fellow, and the mother liked him much. But the daughter refused his invitation, and insulted him into the bargain.

"Even if you had driven in a carriage of brass," she said, "and had offered me a ring set with stones shining as the stars in heaven, I would never have married you—you, a mere peasant!"

The young farmer was terribly upset at her words, and with a prayer for her soul, returned home a saddened man. But her mother scolded and reproached her.

The next night the woman again awoke, and taking her rosary prayed with still greater fervour, that God would bless her child. This time the girl laughed as she slept.

"What can the poor child be dreaming about?" she said to herself: and sighing she prayed for her again. Then she laid her head upon her pillow and tried in vain to sleep. In the morning, when her daughter was dressing, she said: "Well, my dear, you were dreaming again last night, and laughing like a maniac."

"Was I? Listen, I dreamt a nobleman came for me in a silver carriage, and gave me a golden diadem. When I entered the church with him, the people admired and worshipped me more than the Blessed Virgin."

"Ay me, what a terrible dream! what a wicked dream! Pray God not to lead you into temptation."

Then she scolded her daughter severely and went out, slamming the door after her. That same day a carriage drove into the village, and some gentlemen invited mother and daughter to share the bread of the lord of the manor. The mother considered such an offer a great honour, but the daughter refused it and replied to the gentlemen scornfully: "Even if you had come to fetch me in a carriage of solid silver and had presented me with a golden diadem, I would never have consented to be the wife of your lord."

The gentlemen turned away in disgust and returned home; the mother rebuked her severely for so much pride.

"Miserable, foolish girl!" she cried, "pride is a breath from hell. It is your duty to be humble, honest, and sweet-tempered."

The daughter replied by a laugh.

The third night she slept soundly, but the poor woman at her side could not close her eyes. Tormented with dark forebodings, she feared some misfortune was about to happen, and counted her beads, praying fervently. All at once the young sleeper began to sneer and laugh.

"Merciful God! ah me!" cried the poor woman, "what are these dreams that worry her poor brain!"

In the morning she said, "What made you sneer so frightfully last night? You must have had bad dreams again, my poor child."

"Now, mother, you look as if you were going to preach again."

"No, no; but I want to know what you were dreaming about."

"Well, I dreamt some one drove up in a golden carriage and asked me to marry him, and he brought me a mantle of cloth of pure gold. When we came into church, the crowd pressed forward to kneel before me."

The mother wrung her hands piteously, and the girl left the room to avoid hearing her lamentations. That same day three carriages entered the yard, one of brass, one of silver, and one of gold. The first was drawn by two, the second by three, the third by four magnificent horses. Gentlemen wearing scarlet gloves and green mantles got out of the brass and silver carriages, while from the golden carriage alighted a prince who, as the sun shone on him, looked as if he were dressed in gold. They all made their way to the widow and asked for her daughter's hand.

"I fear we are not worthy of so much honour," replied the widow meekly, but when the daughter's eyes fell upon her suitor she recognised in him the lover of her dreams, and withdrew to weave an aigrette of many-coloured feathers. In exchange for this aigrette which she offered her bridegroom, he placed upon her finger a ring set with stones that shone like the stars in heaven, and over her shoulders a mantle

of cloth of gold. The young bride, beside herself with joy, retired to complete her toilette. Meanwhile the anxious mother, a prey to the blackest forebodings, said to her son-in-law, "My daughter has consented to share your bread, tell me of what sort of flour it is made?"

"In our house we have bread of brass, of silver, and of gold; my wife will be free to choose."

Such a reply astonished her more than ever, and made her still more unhappy. The daughter asked no questions, was in fact content to know nothing, not even what her mother suffered. She looked magnificent in her bridal attire and golden mantle, but she left her home with the prince without saying good-bye either to her mother or to her youthful companions. Neither did she ask her mother's blessing, though the latter wept and prayed for her safety.

After the marriage ceremony they mounted the golden carriage and set off, followed by the attendants of silver and brass. The procession moved slowly along the road without stopping until it reached the foot of a high rock. Here, instead of a carriage entrance, was a large cavern which led out into a steep slope down which the horses went lower and lower. The giant *Zémo-tras* (he who makes the earthquakes) closed the opening with a huge stone. They made their way in darkness for some time, the terrified bride being reassured by her husband.

"Fear nothing," said he, "in a little while it will be clear and beautiful."

Grotesque dwarfs, carrying lighted torches, appeared on all sides, saluted and welcomed their King Kovlad as they illumined the road for him and his attendants. Then for the first time the girl knew she had married Kovlad, but this mattered little to her. On coming out from these gloomy passages into the open they found themselves surrounded by large forests and mountains, mountains that seemed to touch the sky. And, strange to relate, all the trees of whatsoever kind, and even the mountains that seemed to touch the sky, were of solid lead. When they had crossed these marvellous mountains the giant Zémo-tras closed all the openings in the road they had passed. They then drove out upon vast and beautiful plains, in the centre of which was a golden palace covered with precious stones. The bride was weary with looking at so many wonders, and gladly sat down to the feast prepared by the dwarfs. Meats of many kinds were served, roast and boiled, but lo! they were of metal—brass, silver, and gold. Every one ate heartily and enjoyed the food, but the young wife, with tears in her eyes, begged for a piece of bread.

"Certainly, madam, with pleasure," answered Kovlad. But she could not eat the bread which was brought, for it was of brass. Then the king sent for a piece of silver bread, still she could not eat it ; and again for a slice of golden bread, that too she was unable to bite. The servants did all they could to get something to their mistress's taste, but she found it impossible to eat anything.

"I should be most happy to gratify you," said Kovlad "but we have no other kind of food."

Then she realised for the first time in whose power she had placed herself, and she began to weep bitterly and wish she had taken her mother's advice.

"It is of no use to weep and regret," said Kovlad,

"you must have known the kind of bread you would have to break here; your wish has been fulfilled."

And so it was, for nothing can recall the past. The wretched girl was obliged henceforth to live underground with her husband Kovlad, the God of Metals, in his golden palace. And this because she had set her heart upon nothing but the possession of gold, and had never wished for anything better.

II

THE LOST CHILD

LONG long ago there lived a very rich nobleman. But though he was so rich he was not happy, for he had no children to whom he could leave his wealth. He was, besides, no longer young. Every day he and his wife went to church to pray for a son. At last, after long waiting, God sent them what they desired. Now the evening before its arrival the father dreamed that its chance of living would depend upon one condition, namely, that its feet never touched the earth until it was twelve years old. Great care was taken that this should be avoided, and when the little stranger came, only trustworthy nurses were employed to look after him. As the years passed on the child was diligently guarded, some- times he was carried in his nurses' arms, sometimes rocked in his golden cradle, but his feet never touched the ground.

Now when the end of the time drew near the father began preparations for a magnificent feast which should be given to celebrate his son's release. One day while these were in progress a frightful noise, followed by most unearthly yells, shook the castle. The nurse dropped the child in her terror and ran to the window: that instant the noises ceased. On turning to take up the boy, imagine her dismay when she found him no longer there, and remembered that she had disobeyed her master's orders.

Hearing her screams and lamentations, all the servants of the castle ran to her. The father soon followed, asking, "What is the matter? What has happened? Where is my child?" The nurse, trembling and weeping, told of the dis- appearance of his son, his only child. No words can tell the anguish of the father's heart. He sent servants in every direction to hunt for his boy, he gave orders, he begged and prayed, he threw away money right and left, he promised everything if only his son might be restored to him. Search was made without loss of time, but no trace of him could be discovered; he had vanished as completely as if he had never existed.

Many years later the unhappy nobleman learnt that in one of the most beautiful rooms of the castle, footsteps, as of some one walking up and down, and dismal groans, were heard every midnight. Anxious to follow the matter up, for he thought it might in some way concern his lost son, he made known that a reward of three hundred gold pieces would be given to any one who would watch for one whole night in the haunted room. Many were willing, but had not the courage to stay till the end; for at midnight, when the dismal groans were heard, they would run away rather than risk their lives for three hundred gold pieces. The poor father was in despair, and knew not how to discover the truth of this dark mystery.

Now close to the castle dwelt a widow, a miller by trade, who had three daughters. They were very poor, and hardly earned enough for their daily needs. When they heard of the midnight noises in the castle and the promised reward, the eldest daughter said, "As we are so very poor we have nothing to lose; surely we might try to earn these three hundred gold pieces by remaining in the room one night. I should like to try, mother, if you will let me."

The mother shrugged her shoulders, she hardly knew what to say; but when she thought of their poverty and the difficulty they had to earn a living she gave permission for her eldest daughter to remain one night in the haunted room. Then the daughter went to ask the nobleman's consent.

"Have you really the courage to watch for a whole night

in a room haunted by ghosts? Are you sure you are not afraid, my good girl?"

"I am willing to try this very night," she replied. "I would only ask you to give me some food to cook for my supper, for I am very hungry."

Orders were given that she should be supplied with everything she wanted, and indeed enough food was given her, not for one supper only, but for three. With the food, some dry firewood and a candle, she entered the room. Like a good housewife, she first lit the fire and put on her saucepans, then she laid the table and made the bed. This filled up the early part of the evening. The time passed so quickly that she was surprised to hear the clock strike twelve, while at the last stroke, footsteps, as of some one walking, shook the room, and dismal groans filled the air. The frightened girl ran from one corner to the other, but could not see any one. But the footsteps and the groans did not cease. Suddenly a young man approached her and asked, "For whom is this food cooked?"

"For myself," she said.

The gentle face of the stranger saddened, and after a short silence he asked again, "And this table, for whom is it laid?"

"For myself," she replied.

The brow of the young man clouded over, and the beautiful blue eyes filled with tears as he asked once more, "And this bed, for whom have you made it?"

"For myself," replied she in the same selfish and indifferent tone.

Tears fell from his eyes as he waved his arms and vanished.

Next morning she told the nobleman all that had happened, but without mentioning the painful impression her answers had made upon the stranger. The three hundred golden crowns were paid, and the father was thankful to have at last heard something that might possibly lead to the discovery of his son.

On the following day the second daughter, having been told by her sister what to do and how to answer the stranger, went to the castle to offer her services. The nobleman willingly agreed, and orders were given that she should be provided with everything she might want. Without loss of time she entered the room, lit the fire, put on the saucepans, spread a white cloth upon the table, made the bed, and awaited the hour of midnight. When the young stranger appeared and asked, "For whom is this food prepared? for whom is the table laid? for whom is the bed made?" she answered as her sister had bidden her, "For me, for myself only."

As on the night before, he burst into tears, waved his arms, and suddenly disappeared.

Next morning she told the nobleman all that had happened except the sad impression her answers had made upon the stranger. The three hundred gold pieces were given her, and she went home.

On the third day the youngest daughter wanted to try her fortune.

"Sisters," said she, "as you have succeeded in earning three hundred gold crowns each, and so helping our dear mother, I too should like to do my part and remain a night in the haunted room."

E

Now the widow loved her youngest daughter more dearly than the others, and dreaded to expose her to any danger; but as the elder ones had been successful, she allowed her to take her chance. So with the instructions from her sisters as to what she should do and say, and with the nobleman's consent and abundant provisions, she entered the haunted room. Having lit the fire, put on the saucepans, laid the table and made the bed, she awaited with hope and fear the hour of midnight.

As twelve o'clock struck, the room was shaken by the footsteps of some one who walked up and down, and the air was filled with cries and groans. The girl looked everywhere, but no living being could she see. Suddenly there stood before her a young man who asked in a sweet voice, "For whom have you prepared this food?"

Now her sisters had told her how to answer and how to act, but when she looked into the sad eyes of the stranger she resolved to treat him more kindly.

"Well, you do not answer me; for whom is the food prepared?" he asked again impatiently, as she made no reply. Somewhat confused, she said, "I prepared it for myself, but you too are welcome to it."

At these words his brow grew more serene.

"And this table, for whom is it spread?"

"For myself, unless you will honour me by being my guest."

A bright smile illumined his face.

"And this bed, for whom have you made it?"

"For myself, but if you have need of rest it is for you."

He clapped his hands for joy and replied, "Ah, that's

right; I accept the invitation with pleasure, and all that you have been so kind as to offer me. But wait, I pray you wait for me; I must first thank my kind friends for the care they have taken of me."

A fresh warm breath of spring filled the air, while at the same moment a deep precipice opened in the middle of the floor. He descended lightly, and she, anxious to see what would happen, followed him, holding on to his mantle. Thus they both reached the bottom of the precipice. Down there a new world opened itself before her eyes. To the right flowed a river of liquid gold, to the left rose high mountains of solid gold, in the centre lay a large meadow covered with millions of flowers. The stranger went on, the girl followed unnoticed. And as he went he saluted the field flowers as old friends, caressing them and leaving them with regret. Then they came to a forest where the trees were of gold. Many birds of different kinds began to sing, and flying round the young stranger perched familiarly on his head and shoulders. He spoke to and petted each one. While thus engaged, the girl broke off a branch from one of the golden trees and hid it in remembrance of this strange land.

Leaving the forest of gold, they reached a wood where all the trees were of silver. Their arrival was greeted by an immense number of animals of various kinds. These crowded together and pushed one against another to get close to their friend. He spoke to each one and stroked and petted them. Meanwhile the girl broke off a branch of silver from one of the trees, saying to herself, "These will serve me as tokens of this wonderful land, for my sisters would not believe me if I only told them of it."

When the young stranger had taken leave of all his friends he returned by the paths he had come, and the girl followed without being seen. Arrived at the foot of the precipice, he began to ascend, she coming silently after, holding on to his mantle. Up they went higher and higher, until they reached the room in the castle. The floor closed up without trace of the opening. The girl returned to her place by the fire, where she was standing when the young man approached.

"All my farewells have been spoken," said he, "now we can have supper."

She hastened to place upon the table the food so hurriedly prepared, and sitting side by side they supped together. When they had made a good meal he said, "Now it is time to rest."

He lay down on the carefully-made bed, and the girl placed by his side the gold and silver branches she had picked in the Mineral Land. In a few moments he was sleeping peacefully.

Next day the sun was already high in the sky, and yet the girl had not come to give an account of herself. The nobleman became impatient; he waited and waited, becoming more and more uneasy. At last he determined to go and see for himself what had happened. Picture to yourself his surprise and joy, when on entering the haunted chamber he saw his long-lost son sleeping on the bed, while beside him sat the widow's beautiful daughter. At that moment the son awoke. The father, overwhelmed with joy, summoned the attendants of the castle to rejoice with him in his new-found happiness.

Then the young man saw the two branches of metal, and said with astonishment, "What do I see? Did you then follow me down there? Know that by this act you have broken the spell and released me from the enchantment. These two branches will make two palaces for our future dwelling."

Thereupon he took the branches and threw them out of the window. Immediately there were seen two magnificent palaces, one of gold, the other of silver. And there they lived happily as man and wife, the nobleman's son and the miller's daughter. And if not dead they live there still.

THE MAID WITH

HAIR OF GOLD

THE MAID WITH HAIR OF GOLD

THERE was once a king so wise and clever that he understood the language of all animals. You shall hear how he gained this power.

One day an old woman came to the palace and said, " I wish to speak to his majesty, for I have something of great importance to tell him."　When admitted to his presence she presented him with a curious fish, saying, " Have it cooked for yourself, and when you have eaten it you will understand all that is said by the birds of the air, the animals that walk the earth, and the fishes that live under the waters."

The king was delighted to know that which every one else was ignorant of, so he rewarded the old woman generously, and told a servant to cook the fish very carefully.

" But take care," said the monarch, " that you do not taste it yourself, for if you do you will be killed."

George, the servant, was astonished at such a threat, and wondered why his master was so anxious that no one else should eat any of the fish.　Then examining it curiously he said, " Never in all my life have I seen such an odd-looking fish ; it seems more like a reptile.　Now where would be the harm if I did take some ?　Every cook tastes of the dishes he prepares."

When it was fried he tasted a small piece, and while taking some of the sauce heard a buzzing in the air and a voice speaking in his ear.

" Let us taste a crumb : let us taste a little," it said.

He looked round to see where the words came from, but there were only a few flies buzzing about in the kitchen.　At the same moment some one out in the yard said in a harsh jerky voice, " Where are we going to settle ? Where ? "

And another answered, " In the miller's barley-field ; ho ! for the miller's field of barley."

When George looked towards where this strange talk came he saw a gander flying at the head of a flock of geese.

"How lucky," thought he; "now I know why my master set so much value on this fish and wished to eat it all himself."

George had now no doubt that by tasting the fish he had learnt the language of animals, so after having taken a little more he served the king with the remainder as if nothing had happened.

When his majesty had dined he ordered George to saddle two horses and accompany him for a ride. They were soon off, the master in front, the servant behind.

While crossing a meadow George's horse began to prance and caper, neighing out these words, "I say, brother, I feel so light and in such good spirits to-day that in one single bound I could leap over those mountains yonder."

"I could do the same," answered the king's horse, "but I carry a feeble old man on my back; he would fall like a log and break his skull."

"What does that matter to you? So much the better if he should break his head, for then, instead of being ridden by an old man you would probably be mounted by a young one."

The servant laughed a good deal upon hearing this conversation between the horses, but he took care to do so on the quiet, lest the king should hear him. At that moment his majesty turned round, and, seeing a smile on the man's face, asked the cause of it.

"Oh nothing, your majesty, only some nonsense that came into my head."

The king said nothing, and asked no more questions, but

he was suspicious, and distrusted both servant and horses ; so he hastened back to the palace.

When there he said to George, "Give me some wine, but mind you only pour out enough to fill the glass, for if you put in one drop too much, so that it overflows, I shall certainly order my executioner to cut off your head."

While he was speaking two birds flew near the window, one chasing the other, who carried three golden hairs in his beak.

"Give them me," said one, "you know they are mine."

"Not at all, I picked them up myself."

"No matter, I saw them fall while the Maid with Locks of Gold was combing out her hair.　At least, give me two, then you can keep the third for yourself."

"No, not a single one."

Thereupon one of the birds succeeded in seizing the hairs from the other bird's beak, but in the struggle he let one fall, and it made a sound as if a piece of metal had struck the ground.　As for George, he was completely taken off his guard, and the wine overflowed the glass.

The king was furious, and feeling convinced that his servant had disobeyed him and had learnt the language of animals, he said, "You scoundrel, you deserve death for having failed to do my bidding, nevertheless, I will show you mercy upon one condition, that you bring me the Maid with the Golden Locks, for I intend to marry her."

Alas, what was to be done ?　Poor fellow, he was willing to do anything to save his life, even run the risk of losing it on a long journey.　He therefore promised to search for the Maid with the Golden Locks : but he knew not where or how to find her.

When he had saddled and mounted his horse he allowed it to go its own way, and it carried him to the outskirts of a dark forest, where some shepherds had left a bush burning. The sparks of fire from the bush endangered the lives of a large number of ants which had built their nest close by, and the poor little things were hurrying away in all directions, carrying their small white eggs with them.

"Help us in our distress, good George," they cried in a plaintive voice; "do not leave us to perish, together with our children whom we carry in these eggs."

George immediately dismounted, cut down the bush, and put out the fire.

"Thank you, brave man: and remember, when you are in trouble you have only to call upon us, and we will help you in our turn." The young fellow went on his way far into the forest until he came to a very tall fir tree. At the top of the tree was a raven's nest, while at the foot, on the ground, lay two young ones who were calling out to their parents and saying, "Alas, father and mother, where have you gone? You have flown away, and we have to seek our food, weak and helpless as we are. Our wings are as yet without feathers, how then shall we be able to get anything to eat? Good George," said they, turning to the young man, "do not leave us to starve."

Without stopping to think, the young man dismounted, and with his sword slew his horse to provide food for the young birds. They thanked him heartily, and said, "If ever you should be in distress, call to us and we will help you at once."

After this George was obliged to travel on foot, and he

walked on for a long time, ever getting further and further into the forest. On reaching the end of it, he saw stretching before him an immense sea that seemed to mingle with the horizon. Close by stood two men disputing the possession of a large fish with golden scales that had fallen into their net.

"'The net belongs to me," said one, "therefore the fish must be mine."

"Your net would not have been of the slightest use, for it would have been lost in the sea, had I not come with my boat just in the nick of time."

"Well, you shall have the next haul I make."

"And suppose you should catch nothing? No; give me this one and keep the next haul for yourself."

"I am going to put an end to your quarrel," said George, addressing them. "Sell me the fish: I will pay you well, and you can divide the money between you."

Thereupon he put into their hands all the money the king had given him for the journey, without keeping a single coin for himself. The fishermen rejoiced at the good fortune which had befallen them, but George put the fish back into the water. The fish, thankful for this unexpected freedom, dived and disappeared, but returning to the surface, said, "Whenever you may need my help you have but to call me, I shall not fail to show my gratitude."

"Where are you going?" asked the fisherman.

"I am in search of a wife for my old master; she is known as the Maid with the Golden Locks: but I am at a loss where to find her."

"If that be all, we can easily give you information,"

answered they. "She is Princess Zlato Vlaska, and daughter of the king whose crystal palace is built on that island yonder. The golden light from the princess's hair is reflected on sea and sky every morning when she combs it. If you would like to go to the island we will take you there for nothing, in return for the clever and generous way by which you made us stop quarrelling. But beware of one thing: when in the palace do not make a mistake as to which is the princess, for there are twelve of them, but only Zlato Vlaska has hair of gold."

When George reached the island he lost no time in making his way to the palace, and demanded from the king the hand of his daughter, Princess Zlato Vlaska, in marriage to the king his master.

"I will grant the request with pleasure," said his majesty, "but only on one condition, namely, that you perform certain tasks which I will set you. These will be three in number, and must be done in three days, just as I order you. For the present you had better rest and refresh yourself after your journey."

On the next day the king said, "My daughter, the Maid with the Golden Hair, had a string of fine pearls, and the thread having broken, the pearls were scattered far and wide among the long grass of this field. Go and pick up every one of the pearls, for they must all be found."

George went into the meadow, which was of great length and stretched away far out of sight. He went down on his knees and hunted between the tufts of grass and bramble from morning until noon, but not a single pearl could he find.

"Ah, if I only had my good little ants here," he cried, "they would be able to help me."

"Here we are, young man, at your service," answered the ants, suddenly appearing. Then they all ran round him, crying out, "What is the matter?   What do you want?"

"I have to find all the pearls lost in this field, and cannot see a single one: can you help me?"

"Wait a little, we will soon get them for you."

He had not to wait very long, for they brought him a heap of pearls, and all he had to do was to thread them on the string.   Just as he was about to make a knot he saw a lame ant coming slowly towards him, for one of her feet had been burned in the bush fire.

"Wait a moment, George," she called out; "do not tie the knot before threading this last pearl I am bringing you."

When George took his pearls to the king, his majesty first counted them to make sure they were all there, and then said, "You have done very well in this test, to-morrow I will give you another."

Early next morning the king summoned George to him and said, "My daughter, the Princess with the Golden Hair, dropped her gold ring into the sea while bathing.   You must find the jewel and bring it me to-day."

The young fellow walked thoughtfully up and down the beach.   The water was pure and transparent, but he could not see beyond a certain distance into its depths, and therefore could not tell where the ring was lying beneath the water.

"Ah, my golden fishling, why are you not here now?

You would surely be able to help me," he said to himself, speaking aloud.

"Here I am," answered the fish's voice from the sea, "what can I do for you?"

"I have to find a gold ring which has been dropped in the sea, but as I cannot see to the bottom there is no use looking."

The fish said, "Fortunately I have just met a pike, wearing a gold ring on his fin.   Just wait a moment, will you?"

In a very short time he reappeared with the pike and the ring.   The pike willingly gave up the jewel.

The king thanked George for his cleverness, and then told him the third task.   "If you really wish me to give the hand of my daughter with the golden hair to the monarch who has sent you here, you must bring me two things that I want above everything: the Water of Death and the Water of Life."

George had not the least idea where to find these waters, so he determined to trust to chance and "follow his nose," as the saying is.   He went first in one direction and then in another, until he reached a dark forest.

"Ah, if my little ravens were but here, perhaps they would help me," he said aloud.

Suddenly there was heard a rushing noise, as of wings overhead, and then down came the ravens calling " Krák, krák, here we are, ready and willing to help you.   What are you looking for?"

"I want some of the Water of Death and the Water of Life: it is impossible for me to find them, for I don't know where to look."

"Krâk, krâk, we know very well where to find some. Wait a moment."

Off they went immediately, but soon returned, each with a small gourd in his beak. One gourd contained the Water of Life, the other the Water of Death.

George was delighted with his success, and went back on his way to the palace. When nearly out of the forest, he saw a spider's web hanging between two fir trees, while in the centre was a large spider devouring a fly he had just killed. George sprinkled a few drops of the Water of Death on the spider; it immediately left the fly, which rolled to the ground like a ripe cherry, but on being touched with the Water of Life she began to move, and stretching out first one limb and then another, gradually freed herself from the spider's web. Then she spread her wings and took flight, having first buzzed these words in the ears of her deliverer: "George, you have assured your own happiness by restoring mine, for without my help you would never have succeeded in recognising the Princess with the Golden Hair when you choose her to-morrow from among her twelve sisters."

And the fly was right, for though the king, on finding that George had accomplished the third task, agreed to give him his daughter Zlato Vlaska, he yet added that he would have to find her himself.

He then led him to a large room and bade him choose from among the twelve charming girls who sat at a round table. Each wore a kind of linen head-dress that completely hid the upper part of the head, and in such a way that the keenest eye could not discover the colour of the hair.

"Here are my daughters," said the king, "but only one among them has golden hair. If you find her you may take her with you ; but if you make a mistake she will remain with us, and you will have to return empty-handed."

George felt much embarrassed, not knowing what course to take.

"Buzz, Buzz, come walk round these young girls, and I will tell you which is yours."

Thus spoke the fly whose life George had saved.

Thus reassured he walked boldly round, pointing at them one after the other and saying, "This one has not the golden hair, nor this one either, nor this. . . ."

Suddenly, having been told by the fly, he cried, "Here we are : this is Zlato Vlaska, even she herself. I take her for my own, she whom I have won, and for whom I have paid the price with many cares. You will not refuse her me this time."

"Indeed, you have guessed aright," replied the king.

The princess rose from her seat, and letting fall her head-dress, exposed to full view all the splendour of her wonderful hair, which seemed like a waterfall of golden rays, and covered her from head to foot. The glorious light that shone from it dazzled the young man's eyes, and he immediately fell in love with her.

The king provided his daughter with gifts worthy of a queen, and she left her father's palace in a manner befitting a royal bride. The journey back was accomplished without any mishaps.

On their arrival the old king was delighted at the sight of Zlato Vlaska, and danced with joy. Splendid and costly preparations were made for the wedding. His majesty then said to George, "You robbed me of the secret of animal language. For this I intended to have your head cut off and your body thrown to birds of prey. But as you have served me so faithfully and won the princess for my bride I will lessen the punishment—that is, although you will be executed, yet you shall be buried with all the honours worthy of a superior officer."

So the sentence was carried out, cruelly and unjustly. After the execution the Princess with the Golden Hair begged the king to make her a present of George's body, and the monarch was so much in love that he could not refuse his intended bride anything.

Zlato Vlaska with her own hands replaced the head on the body, and sprinkled it with the Water of Death. Immediately the separated parts became one again. Upon this she poured the Water of Life, and George returned to life, fresh as a young roebuck, his face radiant with health and youth.

"Ah me! How well I have slept," said he, rubbing his eyes.

"Yes; no one could have slept better," answered the princess, smiling, "but without me you would have slept through eternity."

When the old king saw George restored to life, and looking younger, handsomer, and more vigorous than ever, he too wanted to be made young again. He therefore ordered his servants to cut off his head and sprinkle it with the Life-Giving Water. They cut it off, but he did not come to life again, although they sprinkled his body with all the water that was left. Perhaps they made some mistake in using

the wrong water, for the head and body were joined, but life itself never returned, there being no Water of Life left for that purpose. No one knew where to get any, and none understood the language of animals.

So, to make a long story short, George was proclaimed king, and the Princess with Hair of Gold, who really loved him, became his queen.

THE JOURNEY TO THE
SUN AND THE MOON

THE JOURNEY TO THE SUN AND
THE MOON

THERE were once two young people who loved each other dearly. The young man was called Jean, the girl, Annette. In her sweetness she was like unto a dove, in her strength and bravery she resembled an eagle.

Her father was a rich farmer, and owned a large estate, but Jean's father was only a poor mountain shepherd. Annette did not in the least mind her lover being poor, for he was rich in goodness: nor did she think her father would object to their marrying.

One day Jean put on his best clothes, and went to ask the farmer for his daughter's hand. The farmer listened without interrupting him, and then replied, "If you would marry Annette, go and ask of the Sun why he does not warm the night as well as the day. Then inquire of the Moon why she does not shine by day as well as by night. When you return with these answers you shall not only have my daughter but all my wealth."

These conditions in no way daunted Jean, who placed his hat on the side of his head, and taking a loving farewell of Annette, set out in search of the Sun. On reaching a small town at the close of day, he looked about for a place wherein to pass the night. Some kind people offered him shelter and invited him to sup with them, inquiring as to the object of his journey. When they heard that he was on his way to visit the Sun and Moon, the master of the house begged him to ask the Sun why the finest pear-tree they had in the town had, for several years, ceased to bear fruit, for it used to produce the most delicious pears in the world.

Jean willingly promised to make this inquiry, and the next day continued his journey.

He walked on and on, over mountain and moor, through

valley and dense forest, until he came to a land where there was no drinking water. The inhabitants, when they heard the object of Jean's journey, begged him to ask the Sun and Moon why a well, that was the chief water supply of the district, no longer gave good water. Jean promised to do so, and resumed his journey.

After long and weary wanderings he reached the Sun's abode, and found him about to start on his travels.

"O Sun," said he, "stop one moment, do not depart without first answering a few questions."

"Be quick then and speak, for I have to go all round the world to-day."

"Pray tell me why you do not warm or light the earth by night as well as day?"

"For this simple reason, that if I did, the world and everything upon it would be very soon burnt up."

Jean then put his questions concerning the pear-tree and the well. But the Sun replied that his sister, the Moon, would be able to answer him on those points.

Hardly had the Sun finished speaking before he was obliged to hurry off, and Jean travelled far and fast to meet the Moon. On coming up to her he said, "Would you kindly stop one moment? there are a few questions I should like to ask you."

"Very well, be quick, for the earth is waiting for me," answered she, and stood still at once.

"Tell me, dear Moon, why you do not light the world by day as well as by night? And why you never warm it?"

"Because if I lit up the world by day as well as by night the plants would produce neither fruit nor flower. And

though I do not warm the earth, I supply it with dew, which
makes it fertile and fruitful."

She was then about to continue her course, but Jean,
begging her to stop one moment longer, questioned her about
the pear-tree which had ceased to bear fruit.

And she answered him thus: "While the king's eldest
daughter remained unmarried the tree bore fruit every year.
After her wedding she had a little child who died and was
buried under this tree. Since then there has been neither
fruit nor flower on its branches: if the child be given
Christian burial the tree will produce blossom and fruit as
in the past."

The Moon was just moving off when Jean begged her to
stop and answer one more question, which was, why the
inhabitants of a certain land were unable to obtain from their
well the clear and wholesome water it had formerly poured
forth.

She replied: "Under the mouth of the well, just where
the water should flow, lies an enormous toad which poisons
it continually: the brim of the well must be broken and
the toad killed, then the water will be as pure and wholesome
as formerly."

The Moon then resumed her journey, for Jean had no
more questions to ask her.

He joyfully went back to claim his Annette, but forgot
not to stop on coming to the land where they were short of
water. The inhabitants ran out to meet him, anxious to
know what he had found out.

Jean led them to the well and there explained the instructions he had received from the Moon, at the same time

showing them what to do. Sure enough, right underneath the brim of the well they found a horrible toad which poisoned everything. When they had killed it, the water immediately became pure and transparent, and sweet to the taste as before.

All the people brought Jean presents, and thus laden with riches he again set out. On arriving at the town where grew the unfruitful pear-tree, he was warmly welcomed by the prince, who at once asked if he had forgotten to question the stars about the tree.

"I never forget a promise once made," replied Jean, "but I doubt whether it will be agreeable to your majesty to know the cause of the evil."

He then related all the Moon had said, and when his directions had been carried out they were rewarded by seeing the tree blossom immediately. Jean was loaded with rich gifts, and the king presented him with a most valuable horse, by means of which he reached home very quickly.

Little Annette was wild with joy on hearing of her lover's safe return, for she had wept and suffered much during his absence. But her father's feelings were very different; he wished never to see Jean again, and had, indeed, sent him in search of the Sun with the hope that he might be burnt up by the heat. True it is that "Man proposes and God disposes." Our young shepherd returned, not only safe and sound, but with more knowledge than any of his evil-wishers. For he had learnt why the Sun neither lights nor warms the earth by night as in the day; also why the Moon does not give warmth, and only lights up during the night. Besides all this he had brought with him riches which far exceeded those of his father-in-law, and a steed full of fire and vigour.

So Annette's father could find no fault, and the wedding was celebrated with joy and feasting. Large quantities of roasted crane were eaten, and glasses overflowing with mead were emptied. So beautiful, too, was the music, that for long, long after it was heard to echo among the mountains, and even now its sweet sounds are heard at times by travellers among those regions.

THE DWARF WITH

THE LONG BEARD

THE DWARF WITH THE LONG BEARD

IN a far distant land there reigned a king, and he had an only daughter who was so very beautiful that no one in the whole kingdom could be compared to her. She was known as Princess Pieknotka, and the fame of her beauty spread far and wide. There were many princes among her suitors, but her choice fell upon Prince Dobrotek. She obtained her father's consent to their marriage, and then, attended by a numerous suite, set off with her lover for the church, having first, as was the custom, received her royal parent's blessing. Most of the princes who had been unsuccessful in their wooing of Pietnotka returned disappointed to their own kingdoms: but one of them, a dwarf only seven inches high, with an enormous hump on his back and a beard seven feet long, who was a powerful prince and magician, was so enraged that he determined to have his revenge. So he changed himself into a whirlwind and lay in wait to receive the princess. When the wedding procession was about to enter the church the air was suddenly filled with a blinding cloud of dust, and Pietnotka was borne up high as the highest clouds, and then right down to an underground palace. There the dwarf, for it was he who had worked this spell, disappeared, leaving her in a lifeless condition.

When she opened her eyes she found herself in such a magnificent apartment that she imagined some king must have run away with her. She got up and began to walk about, when lo! as if by some unseen hand the table was laden with gold and silver dishes, filled with cakes of every kind. They looked so tempting, that in spite of her grief she could not resist tasting, and she continued to eat until she was more than satisfied. She returned to the sofa and lay down to rest, but being unable to sleep, she looked first at the door, and then at the lamp burning on the table, then at the door again, and then back to the lamp. Suddenly the door opened of itself, giving entrance to four negroes fully armed, and bearing a golden throne, upon which was seated the Dwarf with the Long Beard. He came close up to the sofa and attempted to kiss the princess, but she struck him such a blow in the face

that a thousand stars swam before his eyes, and a thousand
bells rang in his ears; upon which he gave such a shout, that
the palace walls trembled.   Yet his love for her was so great
that he did his best not to show his anger, and turned away
as if to leave her.   But his feet became entangled in his long
beard, and he fell down, dropping a cap he was carrying in his
hand.   Now this cap had the power of making its wearer
invisible.   The negroes hastened up to their master, and
placing him on his throne bore him out.

Directly the princess found herself alone she jumped off
the sofa, locked the door, and picking up the cap ran to a
mirror to try it on and see how it suited her.   Imagine her
amazement when looking in the glass she saw—nothing at all!
She took off the cap, and behold, she was there again as large
as life.   She soon found out what sort of cap it was, and rejoicing in the possession of such a marvel, put it on her head
again and began to walk about the room.   Soon the door was
burst violently open, and the dwarf entered with his beard tied
up.   But he found neither the princess nor the cap, and so
came to the conclusion that she had taken it.   In a great
rage he began to search high and low; he looked under all the
furniture, behind the curtains, and even beneath the carpets,
but it was all in vain.   Meanwhile the princess, still invisible,
had left the palace and run into the garden, which was very
large and beautiful.   There she lived at her ease, eating the
delicious fruit, drinking water from the fountain, and enjoying
the helpless fury of the dwarf, who sought her untiringly.
Sometimes she would throw the fruit-stones in his face, or
take off the cap and show herself for an instant: then she
would put it on again, and laugh merrily at his rage.

One day, while playing this game, the cap caught in the branches of a gooseberry bush. The dwarf seeing this at once ran up, seized the princess in one hand and the cap in the other, and was about to carry both off when the sound of a war-trumpet was heard.

The dwarf trembled with rage and muttered a thousand curses. He breathed on the princess to send her to sleep, covered her with the invisible cap, and seizing a double-bladed sword, rose up in the air as high as the clouds, so that he might fall upon his assailant and kill him at one stroke. We shall now see with whom he had to deal.

After the hurricane had upset the wedding procession and carried off the princess, there arose a great tumult among those at court. The king, the princess's attendants, and Prince Dobrotek sought her in every direction, calling her by name, and making inquiries of every one they met. At last, the king in despair declared that if Prince Dobrotek did not bring back his daughter, he would destroy his kingdom and have him killed. And to the other princes present he promised that whosoever among them should bring Pietnotka back to him should have her for his wife and receive half of the kingdom. Whereupon they all mounted their horses without loss of time and dispersed in every direction.

Prince Dobrotek, overpowered with grief and dismay, travelled three days without eating, drinking, or sleeping. On the evening of the third day he was quite worn-out with fatigue, and stopping his horse in a field, got down to rest for a short time. Suddenly he heard cries, as of something in pain, and looking round saw an enormous owl tearing a hare with its claws. The prince laid hold of the first hard thing that came to his hand; he imagined it to be a stone, but it was really a skull, and aiming it at the owl, killed the bird with the first blow. The rescued hare ran up to him and gratefully licked his hands, after which it ran away: but the human skull spoke to him and said, " Prince Dobrotek, accept my grateful thanks for the good turn you have done me. I belonged to an unhappy man who took his own life, and for this crime of suicide I have been condemned to roll in the mud until I was the means of saving the life of one of God's creatures. I have been kicked about for seven hundred and seventy years, crumbling miserably on the earth, and without exciting the compassion of a single individual. You have been the means of setting me free by making use of me to save the life of that poor hare. In return for this kindness I will teach you how to call to your aid a most marvellous horse, who during my life belonged to me. He will be able to help you in a thousand ways, and when in need of him you have only to walk out on the moorland without once looking behind you, and to say:

> ' Dappled Horse with Mane of Gold,
> Horse of Wonder !   Come to me.
> Walk not the earth, for I am told
> You fly like birds o'er land and sea.'

Finish your work of mercy by burying me here, so that I may be at rest until the day of judgment. Then depart in peace and be of good cheer."

The prince dug a hole at the foot of a tree, and reverently buried the skull, repeating over it the prayers for the dead. Just as he finished he saw a small blue flame come out of the skull and fly towards heaven : it was the soul of the dead man on its way to the angels.

The prince made the sign of the cross and resumed his journey. When he had gone some way along the moorland he stopped, and without looking back tried the effect of the magic words, saying :

> "Dappled Horse with Mane of Gold,
>   Horse of Wonder !   Come to me.
>   Walk not the earth, for I am told
>   You fly like birds o'er land and sea."

Then amid flash of lightning and roll of thunder appeared the horse. A horse, do I say? Why, he was a miracle of wonder. He was light as air, with dappled coat and golden mane. Flames came from his nostrils and sparks from his eyes. Volumes of steam rolled from his mouth and clouds of smoke issued from his ears. He stopped before the prince, and said in a human voice, "What are your orders, Prince Dobrotek ?"

"I am in great trouble," answered the prince, "and shall be glad if you can help me." Then he told all that had happened.

And the horse said, "Enter in at my left ear, and come out at my right."

The prince obeyed, and came out at the right ear clad in a suit of splendid armour. His gilded cuirass, his steel helmet inlaid with gold, and his sword and club made of him a complete warrior. Still more, he felt himself endowed with superhuman strength and bravery. When he stamped his foot and shouted the earth trembled and gave forth a sound like thunder, the very leaves fell from the trees.

" What must we do?   Where are we to go?" he asked.

The horse replied, "Your bride, Princess Pietnotka, has been carried off by the Dwarf with the Long Beard, whose hump weighs two hundred and eighty pounds.   This powerful magician must be defeated, but he lives a long way from here, and nothing can touch or wound him except the sharp smiting sword that belongs to his own brother, a monster with the head and eyes of a basilisk.   We must first attack the brother."

Prince Dobrotek leaped on to the dappled horse, which was covered with golden trappings, and they set off immediately, clearing mountains, penetrating forests, crossing rivers; and so light was the steed's step that he galloped over the grass without bending a single blade, and along sandy roads without raising a grain of dust.   At last they reached a vast plain, strewn with human bones.   They stopped in front of a huge moving mountain, and the horse said :

" Prince, this moving mountain that you see before you is the head of the Monster with Basilisk Eyes, and the bones that whiten the ground are the skeletons of his victims, so beware of the eyes that deal death.   The heat of the midday sun has made the giant sleep, and the sword with the never-failing blade lies there before him.   Bend down and lie along my neck until we are near enough, then seize the sword and you have nothing more to fear.   For, without the sword, not only will the monster be unable to harm you, but he himself will be completely at your mercy."

The horse then noiselessly approached the huge creature, upon which the prince bent down, and quickly picked up the sword.   Then, raising himself on his steed's back, he gave a

"Hurrah!" loud enough to wake the dead. The giant lifted his head, yawned, and turned his bloodthirsty eyes upon the prince; but seeing the sword in his hand he became quiet, and said, "Knight, is it weariness of life that brings you here?"

"Boast not," replied the prince, "you are in my power. Your glance has already lost its magic charm, and you will soon have to die by this sword. But first tell me who you are."

"It is true, prince, I am in your hands, but be generous, I deserve your pity. I am a knight of the race of giants, and if it were not for the wickedness of my brother I should have lived in peace. He is the horrible dwarf with the great hump and the beard seven feet long. He was jealous of my fine figure, and tried to do me an injury. You must know that all his strength, which is extraordinary, lies in his beard, and it can only be cut off by the sword you hold in your hand. One day he came to me and said, 'Dear brother, I pray you help me to discover the sharp smiting sword that has been hidden in the earth by a magician. He is our enemy, and he alone can destroy us both.' Fool that I was, I believed him, and by means of a large oak tree, raked up the mountain and found the sword. Then we disputed as to which of us should have it, and at last my brother suggested that we should cease quarrelling and decide by lot. 'Let us each put an ear to the ground, and the sword shall belong to him who first hears the bells of yonder church,' said he. I placed my ear to the ground at once, and my brother treacherously cut off my head with the sword. My body, left unburied, became a great mountain, which is now overgrown with forests. As for my head, it is full of a life and strength proof against all dangers, and has remained here ever since to frighten all who attempt to take away the sword. Now, prince, I beg of you, use the sword to cut off the beard of my wicked brother; kill him, and return here to put an end to me: I shall die happy if I die avenged."

"That you shall be, and very soon, I promise you," replied his listener.

The prince bade the Dappled Horse with Golden Mane carry him to the kingdom of the Dwarf with the Long Beard. They reached the garden gate at the very moment when the dwarf had caught sight of Princess Pietnotka and was running after her. The war-trumpet, challenging him to fight, had obliged him to leave her, which he did, having first put on her head the invisible cap.

While the prince was awaiting the answer to his challenge he heard a great noise in the clouds, and looking up saw the dwarf preparing to aim at him from a great height. But he missed his aim and fell to the ground so heavily that his body was half buried in the earth. The prince seized him by the beard, which he at once cut off with the sharp smiting sword.

Then he fastened the dwarf to the saddle, put the beard in his helmet, and entered the palace. When the servants saw that he had really got possession of the terrible beard, they opened all the doors to give him entrance. Without losing a moment he began his search for Princess Pietnotka. For a long time he was unsuccessful, and was almost in despair when he came across her accidentally, and, without knowing it, knocked off the invisible cap. He saw his lovely bride sound asleep, and being unable to wake her he put the cap in his pocket, took her in his arms, and, mounting his steed, set off to return to the Monster with the Basilisk Eyes. The giant swallowed the dwarf at one mouthful, and the prince cut the monster's head up into a thousand pieces, which he scattered all over the plain.

He then resumed his journey, and on coming to the moorland the dappled horse stopped short and said, "Prince, here for the present we must take leave of each other. You are not far from home, your own horse awaits you; but before leaving, enter in at my right ear and come out at my left."

The prince did so, and came out without his armour, and clad as when Pietnotka left him.

The dappled horse vanished, and Dobrotek whistled to his own horse, who ran up, quite pleased to see him again. They immediately set off for the king's palace.

But night came on before they reached the end of their journey.

The prince laid the sleeping maiden on the grass, and, covering her up carefully to keep her warm, he himself fell fast asleep. By chance, a knight, one of her suitors, passed that way. Seeing Dobrotek asleep he drew his sword and stabbed him; then he lifted the princess on his horse and soon reached the king's palace, where he addressed Pietnotka's father in these words: "Here is your daughter, whom I now claim as my wife, for it is I who have restored her to you. She was carried off by a terrible sorcerer who fought with me three days and three nights. But I conquered him, and I have brought you the princess safely back."

The king was overjoyed at seeing her again, but finding

that his tenderest efforts were powerless to awake her, he wanted to know the reason of it.

"That I cannot tell you," replied the impostor; "you see her as I found her myself."

Meanwhile, poor Prince Dobrotek, seriously wounded, was slowly recovering consciousness, but he felt so weak that he could hardly utter these words:

> "Come, Magic Horse with Mane of Gold,
> Come, Dappled Horse, O come to me.
> Fly like the birds as you did of old,
> As flashes of lightning o'er land and sea."

Instantly a bright cloud appeared, and from the midst thereof stepped the magic horse. As he already knew all that had happened, he dashed off immediately to the Mountain of Eternal Life. Thence he drew the three kinds of water: the Water that gives Life, the Water that Cures, and the Water that Strengthens. Returning to the prince, he sprinkled him first with the Life-giving Water, and instantly the body, which had become cold, was warm again and the blood began to circulate. The Water that Cures healed the wound, and the Strength-giving Water had such an effect upon him that he opened his eyes and cried out, "Oh, how well I have slept."

"You were already sleeping the eternal sleep," replied the dappled horse. "One of your rivals stabbed you mortally, and carried off Pietnotka, whom he pretends to have rescued. But do not worry yourself, she still sleeps, and none can arouse her but you, and this you must do by touching her with the dwarf's beard. Go now, and be happy."

The brave steed disappeared in a whirlwind, and Prince

Dobrotek proceeded on his way. On drawing near the capital he saw it surrounded by a large foreign army; part of it was already taken, and the inhabitants seemed to be begging for mercy. The prince put on his invisible cap, and began to strike right and left with the sharp smiting sword. With such fury did he attack the enemy that they fell dead on all sides, like felled trees. When he had thus destroyed the whole army he went, still invisible, into the palace, where he heard the king express the utmost astonishment that the enemy had retired without fighting.

"Where then is the brave warrior who has saved us?" said his majesty aloud.

Every one was silent, when Dobrotek took off his magic cap, and falling on his knees before the monarch, said: "It is I, my king and father, who have routed and destroyed the enemy. It is I who saved the princess, my bride. While on my way back with her I was treacherously killed by my rival, who has represented himself to you as her rescuer, but he has deceived you. Lead me to the princess, that I may awaken her."

On hearing these words the impostor ran away as quickly as possible, and Dobrotek approached the sleeping maiden. He just touched her brow with the dwarf's beard, upon which she opened her eyes, smiled, and seemed to ask where she was.

The king, overcome with joy, kissed her fondly, and the same evening she was married to the devoted Prince Dobrotek. The king himself led her to the altar, and to his son-in-law he gave half his kingdom. So splendid was the wedding banquet, that eye has never seen, nor ear ever heard of its equal.

THE FLYING CARPET, THE INVISIBLE
CAP, THE GOLD-GIVING RING,
AND THE SMITING CLUB

THE FLYING CARPET, THE INVISIBLE CAP, THE GOLD-GIVING RING, AND THE SMITING CLUB

IN a cottage near the high-road, and close to the shores of a large lake, there once lived a widow, poor and old. She was very very poor, but her mother's heart was rich in pride in her son, who was the joy of her life. He was a handsome lad with an honest soul. He earned his living by fishing in the lake, and succeeded so well that neither he nor his mother were ever in want of their daily bread. Every one called him "the fisherman."

One evening at dusk he went down to the lake to throw in his nets, and standing on the shore with a new bucket in his hand, waited to put into it whatever fish it might please God to send him. In about a quarter of an hour or so he drew in his nets and took out two bream. These he threw into the bucket, and humming a merry song turned to go home. At that moment a traveller, poorly clad, with hair and beard white as the wings of a dove, spoke to him, saying, "Have pity on a feeble old man, obliged to lean on his stick, hungry and ragged. I beg you, in Heaven's name, to give me either money or bread. The sun will soon set, and I who have eaten nothing to-day shall have to pass the night fasting, with the bare earth for a bed."

"My good old friend, I am sorry I have nothing about me to give you, but you see the black smoke curling up in the distance? That is our cottage, where my old mother is waiting for me to bring her some fish to cook for our supper. Now take these two bream to her, meanwhile I will return to the lake and throw in my nets again to see if I can catch something more. Thus, with God's help, we shall all three have enough for supper to-night and breakfast to-morrow morning."

While speaking the fisherman handed the fish to the old man, when, marvel of marvels! he melted into the rays of the setting sun and vanished, both he and the fish.

The fisherman, much astonished, rubbed his eyes and looked about on all sides. For a moment he felt afraid, but when he had crossed himself all terror left him and he

went to draw in his nets by the light of the moon. And what
do you think he found in them? It was neither a pike nor
a trout, but a small fish with eyes of diamonds, fins of rain-
bow colour, and golden scales that shone and flashed like
lightning.

When he had spread his nets on the beach the fish began
to talk to him in the language of men.

"Do not kill me, young fisherman," it said, "but accept
in exchange for my life this golden ring. Every time you
put it on your finger repeat these words:

'I conjure thee, O ring, who gold can give,
  In the name of the little fishling of gold,
  For the good of man, that man may live,
  And the honour of heaven, send, new or old,
  Little or much, as may be my need,
  Coins of the realm, let them fall like seed.'

After uttering each of these words, a shower of gold pieces
will fall."

The fisherman gladly accepted the ring, and freeing the
miraculous fish from the net he threw it back into the water.
As it fell, it shone in the air like a shooting star and then
disappeared beneath the waves.

On his way back he said to himself, "My mother and I
will go to bed hungry to-night, without our fried fish, but to-
morrow, when I have made the golden coins gleam in our
humble cottage, all sorts of good things will find their way
there, and we shall live like lords."

But things turned out very differently, for the first thing
he saw on opening the door was the table covered with a

white cloth, and upon it a china soup-tureen in which lay the two bream freshly cooked.

"Where did you get those fish from, dear mother?"

"I do not know myself," replied she, "for I have neither cleaned them nor cooked them. Our table spread itself, the fish placed themselves upon it, and although they have been there an hour they do not get cold; any one might think they had just been taken off the fire. Come, let us eat them."

The widow and her son sat down, said grace, and after eating as much as they wanted went to bed.

Next morning, at breakfast time, the fisherman made the sign of the cross, and then put on the gold ring, at the same time repeating the words the fish had taught him:

> "I conjure thee, O ring, who gold can give,
> In the name of the little fishling of gold,
> For the good of man, that man may live,
> And the honour of heaven, send, new or old,
> Little or much, as may be my need,
> Coins of the realm, let them fall like seed."

When he had ceased speaking the room was filled with a blast of wind followed by flashes of lightning, then a hailstorm of gold pieces showered down and quite covered the table.

The chink of the money aroused his mother, who sat up in bed perfectly amazed.

"What is the meaning of this, my son? Am I awake or dreaming? or is it the work of the Evil One? Where did all that money come from?"

"Fear not, mother, I wear a cross that charms away evil spirits. I have my work, so that you shall never want, and I

have your heart, where for me there will ever be love to sweeten the disappointments and troubles of life. This gold that you see will drive poverty far away, and enable us to help others. Take these pieces, lock them up safely, and use them when in need. As for me, kiss me, and wish me good luck on my journey."

"What! Is it possible that you want to leave me already? Why? and whither are you going?"

"I want to go, mother mine, to see the great city. When there, I mean to enrol myself in the national army. Thus the fisherman turned soldier will become the defender of his king, for the glory of his country and his mother."

"Of a truth, my son, I have heard some talk about the king being in danger, and that our enemies are trying to take his crown from him. But why should you go? Stay at home rather, for alone and unnoticed among so many troops you will neither be able to help nor to hinder."

"You are right, one man alone is a small thing, but by adding one grain to another the measure overflows. If all those who are capable of bearing arms will help the king, there is no doubt that he will soon overcome his enemies."

"But a harmless fisherman like you! Of what use can you be in a battle?"

"The fisherman has, doubtless, a peaceable disposition, and he never boasts of his strength. But when the right moment comes he knows how to handle a sword, and how to water the land with the enemy's blood. And the victorious king will, perhaps, reward me for my bravery by giving me some splendid castle, or a few acres of forest land, a suit of armour and a horse, or even the hand of his daughter in marriage."

“If you feel like this,” answered she, “go, and may God bless you. May He cover you, dear child, with His grace as with a buckler, so that neither guns nor sabres shall do you harm. May He take you under His protection, so that you may return safe and sound to be a comfort to me; and at the end of my days may I rejoice in your happiness, and live near you as long as God in His wisdom shall allow.”

Then she gave him her blessing and kissed him tenderly, making the sign of the cross in the direction he was about to take.

So he departed, and after a few days’ march reached the capital, thinking within himself how he might help the king most effectually.

The town was surrounded by a countless host who threatened to utterly destroy it unless the king would agree to pay a very large ransom.

The people crowded into the square, and stood before the palace gates listening to the herald’s proclamation.

“Hear the king’s will,” said the herald; “listen, all ye faithful subjects, to the words he speaks to you by my mouth. Here are our deadly enemies, who have scattered our troops, and have come to besiege the capital of our kingdom. If we do not send them, by daybreak to-morrow, twenty-four waggons, each drawn by six horses and loaded with gold, they threaten to take the town and destroy it by fire and sword, and to deliver our land to the soldiers. It is certain that we cannot hold out any longer, and our royal treasure-house does not contain one-half the amount demanded. Therefore, through me our sovereign announces, that whosoever among you shall succeed, either in defeating our foes, or in providing the money needed for the ransom, him will he appoint his heir to the crown, and to him will he give his only daughter in marriage, a princess of marvellous beauty. Further, he shall receive half the kingdom in his own right."

When the fisherman heard these words he went to the king and said, "My sovereign and father, command that twenty-four waggons, each harnessed with twenty-four horses and provided with leathern bags, be brought into the court-yard; I will engage to fill them with gold, and that at once, before your eyes."

Then he left the palace, and standing in the middle of the large square, recited the words the fish had taught him.

These were followed by rumblings of thunder and flashes of lightning, and then by a perfect hurricane which sent down masses and showers of gold. In a few minutes the square was covered with a layer of gold so thick that, after loading the twenty-four waggons and filling a large half of the royal treasure-house, there was enough left to make handsome presents to all the king's officers and servants.

Next day the enemy returned to their own country laden with the heavy ransom they had demanded.

The king sent for the fisherman, and inviting him to partake of hydromel wine and sweetmeats, said, "You have to-day been the means of saving our capital from a great calamity, and shall, therefore, receive the reward which you have earned. My only daughter, a princess of great beauty, shall be your wife, and I will give you the half of my kingdom for a wedding present. I also appoint you my heir to the throne. But tell me, to whom am I indebted? What kingdom or land belongs to you? How is it that by a mere movement of the hand you were able to supply my enemies with such a quantity of gold?"

And the fisherman, simple-hearted and straightforward as a child, ignorant of the deceptions practised in court, answered frankly, "Sire, I belong to no royal or princely family, I am a simple fisherman and your loyal subject. I procure my gold by means of this magic ring, and at any time I can have as much as I want."

Then he told how his good fortune had come to him.

The king made no answer, but it hurt his royal dignity to think that he owed his safety to one of his own peasants, and that he had promised to make him his son-in-law.

That evening, after a luxurious supper, the fisherman, having taken a little more wine than usual, ventured to ask the king to present him to his bride. The king whispered a few words in the ear of the chamberlain of the court, and then went out.

The chamberlain took the fisherman to the top of the castle tower, and there said to him, "According to the customs of the court you should, before being introduced to the princess, send her by my hands some valuable jewel as a wedding gift."

"But I have nothing of value or beauty about me," replied he, "unless you offer the princess this golden ring, to which I owe all my good fortune, the princess herself, and the safety of her father."

The chamberlain took the ring, and opening the window of the tower, asked, "Fisherman, do you see the moon in the heavens?"

"I do."

"Very well, she shall be the witness of your betrothal. Now look down; do you see that precipice, and the deep river shining in its depths."

"I do."

"Very well, it shall be your bridal couch."

So saying the chamberlain threw him into the deep abyss, shut the window, and ran to tell the king that there was no longer a suitor for the hand of his daughter.

The fisherman, stunned by the force of his fall, reached the water quite senseless. When he came to himself and opened his eyes, he lay in a boat which at that moment was leaving the mouth of the river and entering the open sea.

The very old man, to whom he had given the bream, was guiding the vessel with an oar.

"My good old man, is it you? How did you manage to save me?" asked the astonished fisherman.

"I came to your assistance," replied the old man, "because he who shows pity to others deserves their help when in need of it. But take the oar and row to whatever place you wish."

And having thus spoken the mysterious old man disappeared. The fisherman crossed himself, and having looked round upon the royal palace sparkling with light he sighed deeply, and chanting the hymn " Under Thy Help," put out to sea.

When the sun rose he saw some nets in the boat, and throwing them into the water caught some pike, which he sold in a town near the shore, and then continued his journey on foot.

Two or three months later, when crossing some open country, he heard cries for help which came from a hill near the forest. There he saw two little demons pulling each other's hair. By the cut of their short waistcoats, by their tight pantaloons and three-cornered hats, he knew that they were inhabitants of the nether world, from which they must have escaped. He had no doubt about it, but being a good Christian he was not afraid, and accosted them boldly, saying, "Why do you ill-treat each other in this way? What is the meaning of it?"

"It means, that for many a long year we have both been working hard to entice a silly fellow down below. He was first tempted by the desire to learn something of sorcery, and he ended by becoming an accomplished scoundrel. After giving him time to commit a great many crimes and thus forfeit his soul, we handed him over to safe keeping. Now we want to divide his property between us. He has left three things, which by every right belong to us. The first is a wonderful carpet. Whoever sits down upon it, and pronounces certain magic words, will be carried off at once, over forests and under clouds, never stopping until his destination is reached. The magic words are as follows :

> 'Carpet, that of thyself through space takes flight,
> O travel, thou airy car, both day and night
> Till my desired haven comes in sight.'

The second piece of property is that club lying on the grass. After uttering some magic words, the club will immediately begin to hit so vigorously that a whole army may be crushed to pieces or dispersed. The words run thus :

> 'Club, thou marvellous club, who knows
> How to strike and smite my foes,
> By thine own strength and in God's name
> O strike well home and strike again.'

The third piece of property is a cap that renders its wearer invisible. Now, my good man, you see our difficulty : there are but two of us, and we are fighting to decide how these three lots may be divided into two equal parts."

" I can help you," said the fisherman, "provided you will do as I tell you. Leave the three lots here just as they are — the carpet, the club, and the magic cap. I will roll a stone from the top of this hill to the bottom—whoever catches it first shall have two lots for his share. What do you say ? "

" Agreed ! " cried the demons, racing after the stone that rolled and bounded on its way down.

In the meantime the fisherman hastily put on the cap, seized the club, and sitting down on the carpet, repeated the magic formula without forgetting a single word.

He was already high up in the air when the demons returned carrying the stone and calling out to him to come and reward the winner.

"Come down and divide those things between us," they cried after him.

The fisherman's only answer was the magic address to his club. This enchanted weapon then fell upon them and struck so hard that the country round echoed to the sound thereof. In the midst of screams and cries and clouds of dust they escaped at last, and the club, of its own accord, came back and placed itself at the fisherman's orders. He, in spite of the rapid motion, sat comfortably on the carpet with the cap under his arm and the club in his hand. Thus they flew over forests, under clouds, and so high that seen from the earth they looked like a tiny white cloud.

Within two or three days they stopped at the king's

capital. The fisherman, with his cap on, descended into the middle of the courtyard.

The whole place was in confusion and trouble, for the commander of the foreign army, encouraged by having so easily received such a large sum of money, had returned to the attack and again held the town in siege, declaring that he would destroy every house and slay all the inhabitants, not sparing even the king himself, unless he agreed to give him his only daughter in marriage.

The terrified citizens crowded to the palace and besought his majesty to do as they asked him, and so save them from such a fate. The king, standing on the balcony, addressed them thus: "Faithful and devoted people, listen to me. Nothing but a miracle can save us from this fearful calamity; yet it has happened that the most powerful assailants have been forced to ask mercy of the most feeble. I will never consent to the marriage of my only daughter with my most hated and cruel foe. Within a few moments my guards will be ready for combat, and I myself will lead them against the enemy. If there be any among you who can win the victory, to him will I give my only daughter in marriage, the half of my kingdom for her dowry, and the heirship to the throne."

When he had finished speaking the fisherman ordered his club to fall on the foe, while the country round echoed and re-echoed to the blows by means of which it destroyed the besieging army. It was in vain that the brave commander shouted to his soldiers not to run away, for when he himself received three blows from the club he was obliged to make off as fast as possible.

When the club had destroyed or driven away into the

desert all the troops it came back to its master; he, still wearing the magic cap, and with his carpet folded up under his arm and his club in his hand, made his way to the king's apartment.

In the palace shouts of joy had succeeded the cries of fear which had been heard but a short while ago. Every one was happy, and every one congratulated the king upon his victory, as sudden and complete as it was unexpected. But the monarch, turning to his warriors, addressed them thus: "Victory! Let us rather return thanks to God. He who has won for us the victory has but to present himself and receive the reward he so richly deserves, that is, my beautiful daughter in marriage, the half of my kingdom, and the right of succession to my throne. These are the gifts that await this victorious hero. Where is he?"

They all stood silent and looked from one to the other. Then the fisherman, who had taken off his cap, appeared before the assembly and said, "Behold, it was I who destroyed your enemies, O king. This is the second time that I have been promised the hand of the princess in marriage, the half of the kingdom, and the right of succession to the throne."

The king, struck dumb with amazement, looked inquiringly at his chamberlain, then recovering his presence of mind he shook hands with the fisherman.

"Your good health, my friend. By what happy fortune do you return safe and sound to my court? The chamberlain told me that through your own carelessness you had fallen out of the tower window; in truth, we mourned you as dead."

"I should not have fallen out of the window if I had not been thrown down by your chamberlain; there is the traitor.

I only escaped death through God's help, and I have just come to the palace in my air-car."

The king made a pretence of being angry with the guilty chamberlain, and ordered his guards to take him away to the donjon cell; then, with pretended friendship, he embraced the fisherman and led him to his own apartments. All the while he was thinking and thinking what he could do to get rid of him. The idea of having him, a mere peasant and one of his own subjects, for a son-in-law was most repugnant to him, and hurt his kingly pride. At last he said, "The chamberlain will most certainly be punished for his crime. As for you, who have twice been my saviour, you shall be my son-in-law. Now the customs observed at court demand that you should send your bride a wedding gift, a jewel, or some other trifle of value. When this has been observed I promise to give my blessing on the marriage, and may you both be happy and live long."

"I have no jewel worthy of the princess's acceptance. I might have given her as much gold as she wished, but your chamberlain took my magic golden ring from me."

"Before insisting upon its return something else might be done. I thoroughly appreciate the value of your marvellous flying carpet—why should not we both sit on it and make an excursion to the Valley of Diamonds? There we can obtain stones of the finest water, such as no one in the world has ever possessed. Afterwards we will return here with your wedding present for my daughter."

The king then opened the window, and the fisherman, spreading out his carpet, repeated the magic words.

Thus they took flight into the air, and after travelling one or two hours began to descend at their destination. It was a valley surrounded on all sides by rocks so steep and so difficult of access, that, except by God's special grace, no mortal man imprisoned there could possibly escape. The ground was strewn with diamonds of the finest quality. The king and fisherman found it easy to make a large collection, picking and choosing, gathering and arranging them upon the carpet. When they had put together all there was room for, the king sat down, and pointing to a large diamond shining at a little distance, said to the fisherman, "There is yet a more splendid one by the stream yonder; run, my son-in-law, and bring it here, it would be a pity to leave it."

The man went for it, while the king, taking advantage of his absence to pronounce the magic words, seated himself on the carpet, which lifted itself up, and floating like an air-car above the forest and under the clouds, descended by one of the palace windows.

His joy knew no bounds, for he now found himself not only free from his enemies and rid of the embarrassing presence of the fisherman, but also the possessor of the richest and most beautiful collection of diamonds in the world;—by his orders they were put away in the caves of the royal treasure-house, and with them the magic ring and the flying carpet.

' Meantime the fisherman had returned with the diamond, and had stood aghast to see the carpet vanishing away in the distance.

Wounded at the ingratitude and indignant at the perversity of a prince for whom he had done so much, he burst into tears.

And, indeed, he had good reason to weep. For he had but to look at the enormous height of the polished rocks to be convinced of the impossibility of climbing them. The vegetation, too, was so scanty that it could only provide him with food for a very short time. He saw but two courses open to him : either to die from starvation, or to be devoured by the monstrous serpents that crawled about in great numbers. Night was now coming on, and the poor fellow was obliged to plan some way of escaping the frightful reptiles which were leaving their hiding-places. At last he climbed up a tree, the highest he could find, and there, with his magic cap on and his club in his hand, passed the night without even closing his eyes.

Next morning when the sun rose the serpents went back to their holes, and the fisherman got down from his tree feeling stiff with cold and very hungry. For some time he walked about the valley in search of food, turning over the diamonds now so useless to him. There he found a few worthless mushrooms, and with such poor food as berries and sorrel leaves, and the water of the valley stream for drink, he lived for some days.

One night when he went to sleep it happened that his cap came off and fell to the ground, whereupon all the reptiles of the place immediately gathered round him. Aroused by their hisses, he awoke to find himself surrounded on all sides and almost in reach of their stings. He immediately seized his club, and had scarcely begun to repeat the magic formula before the weapon set to work to destroy the snakes, while the rocks resounded right and left with the blows. It was as if the monsters were being covered with boiling water, and the noise they made was like that produced by a flock of birds overtaken by a storm. They roared and hissed and twisted themselves into a thousand knots, gradually disappearing one by one. Then the club returned of its own accord to the fisherman's hands, while he returned thanks to God for having delivered him from such a horrible death. At that moment there appeared upon the top of a steep rock his friend, the old man. Overcome with joy at the sight of him, the fisherman called out, "Save me! come to me, my divine protector."

The old man spread out his arms towards him, and having blessed him drew him up, saying, "Now you are free again, hasten to save your king, his daughter your bride, and their kingdom. After he had left you in the valley as food for serpents he was punished for his great crimes by the return of the enemy, who again laid siege to the capital. This happened at the very moment when he was surrounded by his guests, and was boasting of his possession of the air-car, the magic golden ring, and the rest of his evilly acquired riches.

"His foes had consulted Yaga, a wicked sorceress; she advised them to obtain the help of Kostey the magician, who promised his aid in carrying off the princess. When he came he fell in love with the beautiful maiden at first sight, and determined to marry her himself. In order to bring this about he threw the king, the courtiers, and all the inhabitants of the land into a heavy sleep. Then he bore off the princess to his own palace, where she has been shut up and ill-treated because she refuses to have anything to do with him. His castle is situated at the very end of the world, to the west.

There is nothing to hinder you from taking possession of your carpet and ring, they are hidden in the king's treasure-house. Then go with your cap and club and conquer Kostey, rescue the princess, and deliver the king and his subjects."

The fisherman would have thrown himself at the old man's feet to pour out his gratitude, but he suddenly vanished. So he thanked God for all His mercies, put on his invisible cap, and taking his club, made his way towards the capital.

At the end of three days he entered the royal city. All the inhabitants were sleeping the enchanted sleep, from which they were powerless to rouse themselves. The fisherman went straight to the royal treasure-house, took the magic ring and carpet, then seating himself upon the latter and repeating the magic words, away he went like a bird, over rustling forests and under clouds, floating across the blue sky.

After some days of travel he alighted in Kostey's court-yard. Without a moment's delay he folded up his carpet, put the magic cap on his head, and with club in hand entered Kostey's room. There, to his astonishment, stood the magician himself, admiring the wondrous beauty of the princess. For she was perfectly beautiful; eye had never seen nor ear heard of such loveliness. With a low bow full of pride and an ironical smile he was saying to her: "Beauteous princess, you have sworn a most solemn oath to marry none but that man who can solve your six riddles. It is in vain that I strive to guess them. Now there are only two courses open to you: either to release yourself from your vow, putting the riddles aside and consenting to be my wife; or to persist in your vow and thus deliver yourself up to my anger, which you will bitterly regret. I give you three minutes to decide."

Upon hearing these threats the fisherman trembled with rage, and in a low voice whispered the magic words to his club.

This good weapon did not wait for the order to be repeated, but with one bound came down full upon Kostey's forehead. Stunned for a moment by the violence of the blow, the terrible creature rolled upon the ground. Sparks like fireworks sprang from his eyes, and the noise as of a hundred mills seemed to go through his head. Any ordinary mortal would never have opened his eyes again, but Kostey was immortal.

Getting on his feet he pulled himself together, and tried to find out who had thus attacked him. Then the club began to hit him again, and the sound thereof was like unto blows on an empty vault. It seemed to the magician as if showers of boiling water were being poured upon him. He twisted himself about in awful convulsions, and would have liked to bury himself in his palace walls and be turned to stone.

At last, crippled with wounds, he began to hiss like a serpent, and springing forwards breathed upon the princess, filling the air with the poisonous blast.

The maiden tottered and fell, as if dead. Kostey changed himself into a wreath of smoke, and floating out of the window, disappeared in a hurricane.

The fisherman, still invisible, carried the princess into the courtyard of the castle, hoping that the fresh air might restore her to consciousness. He laid her upon the grass, his heart throbbing with hope and fear, and waited anxiously. Suddenly a raven and his nestlings, attracted by the sight of a dead body, and not being able to see the fisherman, came by croaking, The parent bird said to his young ones:

> " Come, children, sharpen claws and beak, krâk, krâk,
>   For here's a feast not far to seek, krâk, krâk,
>   This young girl's corse so white and sleek, krâk, krâk."

One small bird at once settled down on the princess, but the fisherman seized it and took off his cap, so that he could be seen.

"Fisherman," said the father raven, "let go my dear birdling and I will give you anything you want."

"Then bring me some of the Life-Giving Water."

The raven flew away and returned in about an hour, carrying in his beak a tiny bottle of the water. Then he again begged to have his nestling back.

"You shall have it as soon as I have proved that the water is of the right sort."

So saying, he sprinkled the pale face of the princess. She sighed, opened her eyes, and blushing at the sight of a stranger, got up and said, "Where am I? Why, how soundly I have slept!"

"Lovely princess, your sleep might have lasted for ever."

Then he told her his story, how he had been thrown into the river, abandoned in the Valley of Diamonds, and so on, relating at full length all the marvellous events that had taken place.

She listened attentively, then, thanking him for all he had done for her, placed her hand in his and said, "In the garden behind the palace is an apple-tree that bears golden fruit. A guzla that plays of its own accord hangs on its branches, and is guarded day and night by four negroes. Now the music from this guzla has the wonderful power of restoring health to invalids who listen to it, and happiness to those who are sad. That which is ugly becomes beautiful, and charms and enchantments of all kinds are broken and destroyed for ever."

The fisherman put on his invisible cap and went into the garden in search of the negroes. Before going up to them he addressed the magic words to his golden ring, and after a short thunderstorm a shower of gold covered the ground. The negroes, greedy of wealth, threw themselves upon it, snatching from each other handfuls of the golden rain. While thus engaged the fisherman unhooked the guzla from the branches and hurried off into the courtyard with it. There he unfolded his carpet, and sitting down upon it with the princess at his side, flew high up into the air. He had not forgotten to bring with him the cap, the club, and the ring; the princess took care of the guzla.

They floated across the blue sky, above the rustling forests and under the clouds, and in a few days arrived at the palace. There they descended, but the people still lay wrapped in the enchanted sleep, from which they seemed to have no power of awakening.

The silence of the tomb reigned around. Some of the officers were sitting, others standing, all motionless and rigid, and each one in the position he occupied when last awake. The king held a goblet filled with wine, for he had been giving a toast. The chamberlain had his throat half filled with a lying tale, which there had been no time to finish.

One had the end of a joke upon his lips, another a dainty morsel between his teeth, or a tale ready cooked upon his tongue.

And it was the same in all the villages throughout the length and breadth of the land. All the inhabitants lay under the enchanted spell. The labourer held his whip in the air, for he had been about to strike his oxen. The harvesters with their sickles had stopped short in their work. The shepherds slept by their sheep in the middle of the road. The huntsman stood with the powder still alight on the pan of his gun. The birds, arrested in their flight, hung in mid-air. The animals in the woods were motionless. The water in the streams was still. Even the wind slept. Everywhere men had been overtaken in their occupations or amusements. It was a soundless land, without voice or movement; on all sides calm, death, sleep.

The fisherman stood with the princess at his side in the banqueting-hall where slept the king and his guests. Taking the magic guzla from the maid, he pronounced these words:

" O guzla, play, and let thy sweetest harmonies resound
   Through hall and cot, o'er hill and dale, and all the country
      round ;
   That by the power and beauty of thy heavenly tones and song
   Awakened may these sleepers be who sleep too well, too long."

When the first tones of music burst forth everything began to move and live again. The king finished proposing his toast. The chamberlain ended his tale. The guests continued to feast and enjoy themselves. The servants waited at their posts. In short, everything went on just as before, and as if nothing had happened to interrupt it.

And it was just the same in all the country round. Everything suddenly awoke to life. The labourer finished ploughing his furrow. The haymakers built up the hay in ricks. The reapers cut down the golden grain. The hunter's gun went off and shot the duck. The trees rustled. The gardener went on with his work and his song. The rich, who thought only of enjoyment, entertained one another in luxury and splendour.

Now when the king caught sight of his daughter leaning on the fisherman's arm he could hardly believe his own eyes, and it made him very angry. But the princess ran to him, and throwing herself in his arms, related all that he had accomplished. The monarch's heart was softened, and he felt ashamed. With tears in his eyes he drew the fisherman towards him, and before the assembled company thanked him for having the third time saved his life.

"God has punished me for my ill-treatment of you," said he. "Yet He is generous and forgives ; I will fulfil all your wishes."

He then added that the wedding feast should be held that very day, and that his only daughter would be married to the fisherman.

The princess was filled with gladness, and standing with her father's arms round her, said, "I cannot, however, break my word. When in Kostey's palace I made a vow to bestow my hand only on that man who should guess the six riddles I put to him. I am sure the heroic man, who has done so much, will not refuse to submit to this last trial for my sake."

To this the fisherman bowed a willing assent.

The first riddle was: "Without legs it walks. Without arms it strikes. Without life it moves continually."

"A clock," he answered promptly, and to the great satisfaction of the princess, to whom this good beginning seemed to presage a happy ending.

The second riddle ran thus: "Without being either bird, reptile, insect, or any animal whatsoever, it ensures the safety of the whole house."

"A bolt," said her lover.

"Good! Now this is the third: 'Who is that pedestrian who walks fully armed, seasons dishes, and in his sides has two darts? He swims across the water without the help of a boatman.'"

"A lobster."

The princess clapped her hands and begged him to guess the fourth.

"It runs, it moves along on two sides, it has but one eye, an overcoat of polished steel, and a tail of thread."

"A needle."

"Well guessed. Now listen to the fifth: 'It walks without feet, beckons without hands, and moves without a body.'"

"It must be a shadow."

"Exactly," said she, well pleased. "Now you have succeeded so well with these five you will soon guess the sixth: 'It has four feet, but is not an animal. It is provided with feathers and down, but is no bird. It has a body, and gives warmth, but is not alive.'"

"It is certainly a bed," exclaimed the fisherman.

The princess gave him her hand. They both knelt at the king's feet and received his fatherly blessing, after which he with a large wedding party accompanied them to the church. At the same time messengers were sent to bring the fisherman's mother to the palace.

The marvellous guzla played the sweetest music at the marriage feast, while the old king ate and drank and enjoyed himself, and danced like a madman. He treated his guests with so much kindness and generosity that to this very hour the happiness of those who were present is a thing to be talked about and envied.

Now you see what it is to love virtue and pursue it with energy and courage. For by so doing a mere peasant, a poor simple fisherman, married the most lovely and enchanting princess in the whole world. He received, besides, half the kingdom on his wedding day, and the right of succession to the throne after the old king's death.

THE BROAD MAN, THE TALL MAN, AND THE MAN WITH EYES OF FLAME

THE BROAD MAN, THE TALL MAN, AND THE MAN WITH EYES OF FLAME

IT was in those days when cats wore shoes, when frogs croaked in grandmothers' chairs, when donkeys clanked their spurs on the pavements like brave knights, and when hares chased dogs. So you see it must have been a very very long time ago.

In those days the king of a certain country had a daughter, who was not only exceedingly beautiful but also remarkably clever. Many kings and princes travelled from far distant lands, each one with the hope of making her his wife. But she would have nothing to do with any one of them. Finally, it was proclaimed that she would marry that man who for three successive nights should keep such strict watch upon her that she could not escape unnoticed. Those who failed were to have their heads cut off.

The news of this offer was noised about in all parts of the world. A great many kings and princes hastened to make the trial, taking their turn and keeping watch. But each one lost his life in the attempt, for they could not prevent, indeed they were not even able to see, the princess take her flight.

Now it happened that Matthias, prince of a royal city, heard of what was going on and resolved to watch through the three nights. He was young, handsome as a deer, and brave as a falcon. His father did all he could to turn him from his purpose: he used entreaties, prayers, threats, in fact he forbade him to go, but in vain, nothing could prevent him. What could the poor father do? Worn-out with contention, he was at last obliged to consent. Matthias filled his purse with gold, girded a well-tried sword to his side, and quite alone started off to seek the fortune of the brave.

Walking along next day, he met a man who seemed hardly able to drag one leg after the other.

"Whither are you going?" asked Matthias.

"I am travelling all over the world in search of happiness."

"What is your profession?"

"I have no profession, but I can do what no one else can. I am called *Broad*, because I have the power of swelling myself out to such a size that there is room for a whole regiment of soldiers inside me."

So saying he puffed himself out till he formed a barricade from one side of the road to the other.

"Bravo!" cried Matthias, delighted at this proof of his capacities. "By the way, would you mind coming with me? I, too, am travelling across the world in search of happiness."

"If there is nothing bad in it I am quite willing," answered Broad. And they continued their journey together.

A little further on they met a very slender man, frightfully thin, and tall and straight as a portico.

"Whither are you going, good man?" asked Matthias, filled with curiosity at his strange appearance.

"I am travelling about the world."

"To what profession do you belong?"

"To no profession, but I know something every one else is ignorant of. I am called *Tall*, and with good reason. For without leaving the earth I can stretch out and reach up to the clouds. When I walk I clear a mile at each step."

Without more ado he lengthened himself out until his head was lost in the clouds, while he really cleared a mile at each step.

"I like that, my fine fellow," said Matthias. "Come, would you not like to travel with us?"

"Why not?" replied he. "I'll come."

So they proceeded on their way together. While passing through a forest they saw a man placing trunks of trees one upon another.

"What are you trying to do there?" asked Matthias, addressing him.

"I have *Eyes of Flame*," said he, "and I am building a

pile here." So saying he fixed his flaming eyes upon the wood, and the whole was instantly set alight.

"You are a very clever and powerful man," said Matthias, "would you like to join our party?"

"All right, I am willing."

So the four travelled along together. Matthias was over-joyed to have met with such gifted companions, and paid their expenses generously, without complaining of the enormous sum of money he had to spend on the amount of food Broad consumed.

After some days they reached the princess's palace. Matthias had told them the object of his journey, and had promised each a large reward if he was successful. They gave him their word to work with a will at the task which every one up till then had failed to accomplish. The prince bought them each a handsome suit of clothes, and when they were all presentable sent them to tell the king, the princess's father, that he had come with his attendants to watch three nights in the lady's boudoir. But he took very good care not to say who he was, nor whence he had come.

The king received them kindly, and after hearing their request said: "Reflect well before engaging yourselves in this, for if the princess should escape you will have to die."

"We very much doubt her escaping from us," they replied, "but come what will, we intend to make the attempt and to begin at once."

"My duty was to warn you," replied the monarch, smiling, "but if you still persist in your resolution I myself will take you to the lady's apartments."

Matthias was dazzled at the loveliness of the royal maiden,

while she, on her side, received the brilliant and handsome young man most graciously, not trying to hide how much she liked his good looks and gentle manner. Hardly had the king retired when Broad lay down across the threshold; Tall and the Man with Eyes of Flame placed themselves near the window; while Matthias talked with the princess, and watched her every movement attentively.

Suddenly she ceased to speak, then after a few moments said, "I feel as if a shower of poppies were falling on my eyelids."

And she lay down on the couch, pretending to sleep.

Matthias did not breathe a word. Seeing her asleep he sat down at a table near the sofa, leaned his elbows upon it, and rested his chin in the hollow of his hands. Gradually he felt drowsy and his eyes closed, as did those of his companions.

Now this was the moment the princess was waiting for. Quickly changing herself into a dove, she flew towards the window. If it had not happened that one of her wings touched Tall's hair he would not have awakened, and he would certainly never have succeeded in catching her if it had not been for the Man with Eyes of Flame, for he, as soon as he knew which direction she had taken, sent such a glance after her, that is, a flame of fire, that in the twinkling of an eye her wings were burnt, and having been thus stopped, she was obliged to perch on the top of a tree. From thence Tall reached her easily, and placed her in Matthias' hands, where she became a princess again. Matthias had hardly awakened out of his sleep.

Next morning and the morning after the king was greatly

astonished to find his daughter sitting by the prince's side, but he was obliged to keep silent and accept facts as they were, at the same time entertaining his guests royally. At the approach of the third night he spoke with his daughter, and begged her to practise all the magic of which she was capable, and to act in such a way as to free him from the presence of intruders of whom he knew neither the rank nor the fortune.

As for Matthias, he used every means in his power to bring about a happy ending to such a hitherto successful undertaking. Before entering the princess's apartments he took his comrades aside and said, "There is but one more stroke of luck, dear friends, and then we have succeeded. If we fail, do not forget that our four heads will roll on the scaffold."

"Come along," replied the three; "never fear, we shall be able to keep good watch."

When they came into the princess's room they hastened to take up their positions, and Matthias sat down facing the lady. He would have much preferred to remain with her without being obliged to keep watch all the time for fear of losing her for ever. Resolving not to sleep this time, he said to himself, "Now I will keep watch upon you, but when you are my wife I will rest."

At midnight, when sleep was beginning to overpower her watchers, the princess kept silence, and, stretching herself on the couch, shut her beautiful eyes as if she were really asleep.

Matthias, his elbows on the table, his chin in the palms of his hand, his eyes fixed upon her, admired her silently. But as sleep closes even the eyes of the eagle, so it shut those of the prince and his companions.

The princess, who all this time had been watching them

narrowly and only waiting for this moment, got up from her seat, and changing herself into a little fly, flew out of the window. Once free, she again changed herself into a fish, and falling into the palace well, plunged and hid herself in the depths of the water.

She would certainly have made her escape if, as a fly, she had not just touched the tip of the nose of the Man with Eyes of Flame. He sneezed, and opened his eyes in time to notice the direction in which she had disappeared. Without losing an instant he gave the alarm, and all four ran into the courtyard. The well was very deep, but that did not matter. Tall soon stretched himself to the required depth, and searched in all the corners : but he was unable to find the little fish, and it seemed impossible that it could ever have been there.

" Now then, get out of that, I will take your place," said Broad.

And getting in at the top by the rim, he filled up all the inside of the well, stopping it so completely with his huge body that the water sprang out : but nothing was seen of the little fish.

" Now it is my turn," said the Man with Eyes of Flame. " I warrant I'll dislodge this clever magician."

When Broad had cleared the well of his enormous person the water returned to its place, but it soon began to boil from the heat of the eyes of flame. It boiled and boiled, till it boiled over the rim ; then, as it went on boiling and rising ever higher and higher, a little fish was seen to throw itself out on the grass half cooked. As it touched the ground it again took the form of the princess.

Matthias went to her and kissed her tenderly.

"You have conquered, my master and husband," she said, "you have succeeded in preventing my escape. Henceforth I am yours, both by right of conquest and of my own free will."

The young man's courtesy, strength, and gentleness, as well as his beauty, were very pleasing to the princess; but her father, the king, was not so ready to approve of her choice, and he resolved not to let her go with them. But this did not trouble Matthias, who determined to carry her off, aided by his three comrades. They soon all left the palace.

The king was furious, and ordered his guards to follow them and bring them back under pain of death. Meanwhile Matthias, the princess, and the three comrades had already travelled a distance of some miles. When she heard the steps of the pursuers she begged the Man with Eyes of Flame to see who they were. Having turned to look, he told her that a large army of men on horseback were advancing at a gallop.

"They are my father's guards," said she, "we shall have some difficulty in escaping them."

Then, seeing the horsemen draw nearer she took the veil from her face, and throwing it behind her in the direction of the wind, said, "I command as many trees to spring up as there are threads in this veil."

Instantly, in the twinkling of an eye, a high thick forest rose up between them. Before the soldiers had time to clear for themselves a pathway through this dense mass, Matthias and his party had been able to get far ahead, and even to take a little rest.

"Look," said the princess, "and see if they are still coming after us."

The Man with Eyes of Flame looked back, and replied that the king's guards were out of the forest and coming towards them with all speed.

"They will not be able to reach us," cried she. And she let fall a tear from her eyes, saying as she did so, "Tear, become a river."

At the same moment a wide river flowed between them and their pursuers, and before the latter had found means of crossing it, Matthias and his party were far on in front.

"Man with Eyes of Flame," said the princess, "look behind and tell me how closely we are followed."

"They are quite near to us again," he replied, "they are almost upon our heels."

"Darkness, cover them," said she.

At these words Tall drew himself up. He stretched and stretched and stretched until he reached the clouds, and there, with his hat he half covered the face of the sun. The side towards the soldiers was black as night, while Matthias and his party, lit up by the shining half, went a good way without hindrance.

When they had travelled some distance, Tall uncovered the sun, and soon joined his companions by taking a mile at each step. They were already in sight of Matthias' home, when they noticed that the royal guards were again following them closely.

"Now it is my turn," said Broad; "go on your way in safety, I will remain here. I shall be ready for them."

He quietly awaited their arrival, standing motionless, with his large mouth open from ear to ear. The royal army, who were determined not to turn back without having taken the princess, advanced towards the town at a gallop. They had decided among themselves that if it resisted they would lay siege to it.

Mistaking Broad's open mouth for one of the city gates, they all dashed through and disappeared.

Broad closed his mouth, and having swallowed them, ran to rejoin his comrades in the palace of Matthias' father. He felt somewhat disturbed with a whole army inside him, and the earth groaned and trembled beneath him as he ran. He could hear the shouts of the people assembled round Matthias, as they rejoiced at his safe return.

"Ah, here you are at last, brother Broad," cried Matthias, directly he caught sight of him. "But what have you done with the army? Where have you left it?"

"The army is here, quite safe," answered he, patting his enormous person. "I shall be very pleased to return them as they are, for the morsel is not very easy to digest."

"Come then, let them out of their prison," said Matthias, enjoying the joke, and at the same time calling all the inhabitants to assist at the entertainment.

Broad, who looked upon it as a common occurrence, stood in the middle of the palace square, and putting his hands to his sides, began to cough. Then—it was really a sight worth seeing—at each cough horsemen and horses fell out of his mouth, one over the other, plunging, hopping, jumping, trying who could get out of the way the quickest. The last one had a little difficulty in getting free, for he somehow got into one of Broad's nostrils and was unable to move. It was only by giving a good sneeze that Broad could release him, the last of the royal cavaliers, and he

lost no time in following his companions at the top of his speed.

A few days later a splendid feast was given at the wedding of Prince Matthias and the princess. The king, her father, was also present. Tall had been sent to invite him. Owing to his knowledge of the road and the length of his limbs, he accomplished the journey so quickly that he was there before the royal horsemen had time to get back. It was well for them that it was so, for, had he not pleaded that their lives might be saved, their heads would certainly have been cut off for returning empty-handed.

Everything was now arranged to everybody's satisfaction. The princess's father was delighted to know that his daughter was married to a rich and noble prince, and Matthias generously rewarded his brave travelling companions, who remained with him to the end of their days.

THE HISTORY OF PRINCE SLUGOBYL

OR

THE INVISIBLE KNIGHT

THE HISTORY OF PRINCE SLUGOBYL; OR,
THE INVISIBLE KNIGHT

THERE was once a king who had an only son, called
Prince Slugobyl. Now this young prince loved nothing
better than travelling; so fond of it was he that when he was

twenty years old he gave his father no rest until he allowed him to go on a long journey, in short, to travel all over the world. Thus he hoped to see many beautiful and strange things, to meet with marvellous adventures, to gain happiness, knowledge, and wisdom, and to return a better man in every way than when he left. Fearing his youth and want of experience might lead him astray, his father sent with him a valued and faithful servant. When all was ready, Slugobyl bade the king adieu and set off to visit the land of his dreams.

As he was jogging along, allowing his horse to go at its own pace, he saw a beautiful white swan pursued by an eagle about to pounce down upon it. Seizing his crossbow, he took such good aim that the eagle fell dead at his feet. The rescued swan stopped in its flight, and turning round said to him, "Valiant Prince Slugobyl, it is not a mere swan who thanks you for your most timely help, but the daughter of the Invisible Knight, who, to escape the pursuit of the giant Kostey, has changed herself into a swan. My father will gladly be of service to you in return for this kindness to me. When in need of his help, you only have to say three times, 'Invisible Knight, come to me.'"

Having thus spoken the swan flew away. The prince looked after her for a long time, and then continued his journey. He travelled on and on and on, over high mountains, through dark forests, across barren deserts, and so to the middle of a vast plain where every green thing had been burnt up by the rays of the sun. Not a single tree, not even a bush or a plant of any kind was to be seen. No bird was heard to sing, no insect to hum, no breath of air to stir the stillness of this land of desolation. Having ridden for some hours, the prince began to suffer terribly from thirst; so, sending his servant in one direction, he himself went in another, in search of some well or spring. They soon found a well full of cool fresh water, but unluckily without either rope or bucket to draw it up. After a few moments' thought the prince said to his servant, "Take the leathern strap used for tethering our horses, put it round your body, and I will then let you down into the well; I cannot endure this thirst any longer."

"Your highness," answered the servant, "I am heavier than you, and you are not as strong as I, so you will not be able to pull me out of the water. If you, therefore, will go down first, I shall be able to pull you up when you have quenched your thirst."

The prince took his advice, and fastening an end of the strap under his arms, was lowered into the well. When he had enjoyed a deep draught of the clear water and filled a bottle of the same for his servant, he gave the signal that he wished to be pulled up. But instead of obeying the servant said, "Listen, prince; from the day you were born up to the present moment you have never known anything but luxury, pleasure, and happiness, while I have suffered poverty and slaved all my life. Now we will change places, and you shall be my servant. If you refuse you had better make your peace with God, for I shall drown you."

"Stop, faithful servant," cried the prince, "you will not be so wicked as to do that. What good will it do you? You will never be so happy as you have been with me, and you know what dreadful tortures are in store for murderers in the other world; their hands are plunged into boiling pitch, their shoulders bruised with blows from red-hot iron clubs, and their necks sawn with wooden saws."

"You may cut and saw me as much as you like in the other world," said the servant, "but I shall drown you in this." And he began to let the strap slide through his fingers.

"Very well," said the prince, "I agree to accept your terms. "You shall be the prince and I will be your servant, I give you my word."

"I have no faith in words that are carried away by the first wind that blows. Swear to confirm your promise in writing."

"I swear."

The servant then let down paper and pencil, and dictated the following:

"I hereby declare that I renounce my name and rights in favour of the bearer of this writing, and that I acknowledge him to be my prince, and that I am his servant. Written in the well.   (Signed)   PRINCE SLUGOBYL."

The man having taken this document, which he was quite unable to read, drew out the prince, took off the clothes in which he was dressed, and made him wear those he himself had just taken off. Thus disguised they travelled for a week, and arriving at a large city, went straight to the king's palace. There the false prince dismissed his pretended servant to the stables, and presenting himself before the king, addressed him thus in a very haughty manner:

"King, I am come to demand the hand of your wise and beautiful daughter, whose fame has reached my father's court. In exchange I offer our alliance, and in case of refusal, war."

"Prayers and threats are equally out of place," answered the

king; "nevertheless, prince, as proof of the esteem in which I hold the king, your father, I grant your request: but only on one condition, that you deliver us from a large army that now besets our town. Do this, and my daughter shall be yours."

"Certainly," said the impostor, "I can soon get rid of them, however near they may be. I undertake by to-morrow morning to have freed the land entirely of them."

In the evening he went to the stables, and calling his pretended servant, saluted him respectfully and said, " Listen, my dear friend, I want you to go immediately outside the town and destroy the besieging army that surrounds it. But do it in such a way that every one will believe that I have done it. In exchange for this favour I promise to return the writing in which you renounced your title of prince and engaged to serve me."

The prince put on his armour, mounted his horse, and rode outside the city gates. There he stopped and called three times to the Invisible Knight.

"Behold me, prince, at your service," said a voice close to him. "I will do anything you wish, for you saved my only daughter from the hands of the giant Kostey; I shall always be grateful."

Slugobyl showed him the army he had to destroy before morning, and the Invisible Knight whistled and sang:

> " Magu, Horse with Golden Mane,
> I want your help yet once again,
> Walk not the earth but fly through space
> As lightnings flash or thunders race.
> Swift as the arrow from the bow,
> Come quick, yet so that none can know."

At that instant a magnificent grey horse appeared out of a whirlwind of smoke, and from his head there hung a golden mane. Swift as the wind was he, flames of fire blazed forth from his nostrils, lightnings flashed from his eyes, and volumes of smoke came from his ears. The Invisible Knight leapt upon his back, saying to the prince, "Take my sword and destroy the left wing of the army, while I attack the right wing and the centre."

The two heroes rushed forward and attacked the invaders with such fury that on all sides men fell like chopped wood or dried grass. A frightful massacre followed, but it was in vain that the enemy fled, for the two knights seemed to be everywhere. Within a short time only the dead and dying remained on the battle-field, and the two conquerors quietly returned to the town. On reaching the palace steps, the Invisible Knight melted into the morning mist, and the serving-man prince returned to the stables.

That same night it happened that the king's daughter, not being able to sleep, had remained on her balcony and seen and heard all that had taken place. She had overheard the conversation between the impostor and the real prince, had seen the latter call to his assistance the Invisible Knight, and then doff his royal armour in favour of the false prince; she had seen and understood everything, but she determined to keep silence for a little longer.

But when on the next day the king, her father, celebrated the victory of the false prince with great rejoicings, loaded him with honours and presents, and calling his daughter expressed a wish that she should marry him—the princess could be silent no longer. She walked up to the real prince, who was waiting at table with the other servants, took his arm, and leading him to the king, said:

"Father, and all good people, this is the man who has saved our country from the enemy, and whom God has destined to be my husband. He to whom you pay these honours is but a vile impostor, who has robbed his master of name and rights. Last night I witnessed such deeds as eye has never seen nor ear heard, but which shall be told afterwards. Bid this traitor show the writing which proves the truth of what I say."

When the false prince had delivered up the paper signed by the serving-man prince, it was found to contain the following words:

"The bearer of this document, the false and wicked servant of the serving-man prince, shall receive the punishment his sin deserves.   (Signed)   PRINCE SLUGOBYL."

"What? Is that the real meaning of that writing?" asked the traitor, who could not read.

"Most assuredly," was the reply.

Then he threw himself at the king's feet and begged for mercy. But he received his punishment, for he was tied to the tails of four wild horses and torn to pieces.

Prince Slugobyl married the princess. It was a magnificent wedding. I myself was there, and drank of the mead and wine; but they only touched my beard, they did not enter my mouth.

THE SPIRIT OF

THE STEPPES

THE SPIRIT OF THE STEPPES

IN ancient days there lived a king
and queen; the former was old but
the latter young. Although they loved
one another dearly they were very unhappy, for God had not given them
any children. They fretted and grieved
about this so deeply that the queen
became ill with melancholy. The
doctors advised her to travel. The
king was obliged to remain at home,
so she went without him, accompanied
by twelve maids of honour, all beautiful
and fresh as flowers in May. When
they had travelled for some days, they
reached a vast uninhabited plain which
stretched so far away it seemed to
touch the sky. After driving hither
and thither for some time the driver was
quite bewildered, and stopped before a

large stone column.   At its foot stood a warrior on horseback, clad in steel armour.

"Brave knight, can you direct me to the high-road?" said the driver; "we are lost, and know not which way to go."

"I will show you the way," said the warrior, "but only on one condition, that each of you gives me a kiss."

The queen looked at the warrior in wrath, and ordered the coachman to drive on. The carriage continued moving nearly all day, but as if bewitched, for it always returned to the stone column. This time the queen addressed the warrior.

"Knight," said she, "show us the road, and I will reward you richly."

"I am the Master Spirit of the Steppes," answered he. "I demand payment for showing the way, and my payment is always in kisses."

"Very well, my twelve maids of honour shall pay you."

"Thirteen kisses are due to me; the first must be given by the lady who addresses me."

The queen was very angry, and again the attempt was made to find their way. But the carriage, though during the whole time it moved in an opposite direction, still returned to the stone column. It was now dark, and they were obliged to think of finding shelter for the night, so the queen was obliged to give the warrior his strange payment. Getting out of her carriage she walked up to the knight, and looking modestly down allowed him to kiss her; her twelve maids of honour who followed did the same. A moment later stone column and horseman had vanished, and they found themselves on the high-road, while a perfumed cloud seemed to float over the steppes. The queen stepped into her carriage with her ladies, and so the journey was continued.

But from that day the beautiful queen and her maids became thoughtful and sad; and, losing all pleasure in travel, went back to the capital. Yet the return home did not make the queen happy, for always before her eyes she saw the Horseman of the Steppes. This displeased the king, who became gloomy and ill-tempered.

One day while the king was on his throne in the council chamber he suddenly heard the sweetest warblings, like unto those produced by a bird of paradise; these were answered by the songs of many nightingales. Wondering, he sent to find out what it was. The messenger returned saying that the queen and her twelve maids of honour had each been presented with a girl baby, and that the sweet warblings were but the crying of the children. The king was greatly astonished, and while he was engaged in deep thought about the matter the palace was suddenly lit up by lights of dazzling brightness. On inquiring into the cause he learnt that the little princess had opened her eyes, and that they shone with matchless brilliancy.

At first the king could not speak, so amazed was he. He laughed and he cried, he sorrowed and he rejoiced, and in the midst of it all a deputation of ministers and senators was announced. When these were shown into his presence they fell on their knees, and striking the ground with their foreheads, said, "Sire, save your people and your royal person. The queen and her twelve maids of honour have been presented by the Spirit of the Steppes with thirteen girl babies. We beseech you to have these children killed, or we shall all be destroyed."

The king, roused to anger, gave orders that all the babies should be thrown into the sea. The courtiers were already on their way to obey this cruel command when the queen entered, weeping, and pale as death. She threw herself at the king's feet and begged him to spare the lives of these helpless and innocent children, and instead to let them be placed on a desert island and there left in the hands of God.

The king granted her wish. The baby princess was placed in a golden cradle, her little companions in copper cradles, and the thirteen were taken to a desert island and left quite alone. Every one at court thought that they had perished, and said one to another, "They will die from cold and hunger; they will be devoured by wild beasts, or birds of prey; they are sure to die; perchance they will be buried under dead leaves or covered with snow." But happily nothing of the kind happened, for God takes care of little children.

The small princess grew bigger day by day. Every morning she was awakened by the rising sun, and bathed by the dew. Soft breezes refreshed her, and twisted into plaits her luxuriant hair. The trees sang her to sleep with their rustling lullabies, the stars watched over her at night. The swans clothed her in their soft raiment, and the bees fed her with their honey. The beauty of the little maiden increased with her growth. Her brow was calm and pure as the moon, her lips red as a rosebud, and so eloquent that her voice sounded like a shower of pearls. But wonderful beyond compare was the expressive beauty of her eyes, for if she looked at you kindly you seemed to float in a sea of joy, if

angrily it made you numb with fear, and you were instantly changed into a block of ice. She was waited upon by her twelve companions, who were almost as charming as their mistress, to whom they were devotedly attached. Rumours of the loveliness of Princess Sudolisu spread far and wide. People came to see her from all parts of the world, so that it was soon no longer a desert island, but a thickly populated and magnificent city.

Many a prince came from afar and entered the lists as suitor for the hand of Sudolisu, but none succeeded in winning her love. Those who bore with good temper and resignation the disappointment of being refused returned home safe and sound, but woe to the unlucky wretch who rebelled against her will and attempted to use an armed force; his soldiers perished miserably, while he, frozen to the heart by her angry glance, was turned into a block of ice.

Now it happened that the famous ogre, Kostey, who lived underground, was a great admirer of beauty. And he took it into his head to see what the creatures above ground were doing. By the help of his telescope he was able to observe all the kings and queens, princes and princesses, gentlemen and ladies, living on the earth. As he was looking his eye fell upon a beautiful island, where, bright as many stars, stood twelve maidens; while in their midst, upon a couch of swan's-down, slept a young princess lovely as the dawn of day. Sudolisu was dreaming of a young knight who rode a spirited horse; on his breast was a golden cuirass, and in his hand an invisible club. And in her dream she admired this knight, and loved him more than life itself. The wicked Kostey longed to have her for his own, and determined to carry her off. He reached the earth by striking it from underground three times with his forehead. The princess called her army together, and putting herself at its head, led her soldiers against him. But he merely breathed upon the soldiers and they fell down in an overpowering sleep. Then he stretched out his bony hands to take the princess, but she, throwing a glance full of anger and disdain at him, changed him into a block of ice. Then she shut herself up in her palace. Kostey did not remain frozen long; when the princess had departed he came to life again, and started off in pursuit of her. On reaching the town where she dwelt, he put all the inhabitants into a charmed sleep, and laid the same spell upon the twelve maids of honour. Fearing the power of her eyes, he dared not attack Sudolisu herself; so he surrounded her palace with an iron wall, and left it in charge of a monster dragon with twelve heads. Then he waited, in hope that the princess would give in.

Days passed, weeks grew into months, and still Princess Sudolisu's kingdom looked like one large bedchamber. The people snored in the streets, the brave army lying in the fields slept soundly, hidden in the long grass under the shadow of nettle, wormwood, and thistle, rust and dust marring the brightness of their armour. Inside the palace everything was the same. The twelve maids of honour lay motionless. The princess alone kept watch, silent amid this reign of sleep. She walked up and down her narrow prison, sighing and weeping bitter tears, but no other sound broke the silence; only Kostey, avoiding her glance, still called through the doors and begged her to refuse him no longer. Then he promised she should be Queen of the Nether World, but she answered him not.

Lonely and miserable, she thought of the prince of her dreams. She saw him in his golden armour, mounted on his spirited steed, looking at her with eyes full of love. So she imagined him day and night.

Looking out of window one day, and seeing a cloud floating on the horizon, she cried :

> " Floating Cloudlet soft and white,
>   Pilgrim of the sky,
>   I pray you for one moment, light
>   On me your pitying eye.
>   Where my love is can you tell ?
>   Thinks he of me ill or well ? "

" I know not," answered the cloud, "ask the wind."

Then she saw a tiny breeze playing among the field flowers, and called out :

> " Gentle Breezelet, soul of air,
>   Look not lightly on my pain ;
>   Kindly lift me from despair,
>   Help me freedom to regain.
>   Where my love is can you tell ?
>   Thinks he of me ill or well ? "

" Ask that little star yonder," answered the breeze, "she knows more than I."

Sudolisu raised her beautiful eyes to the twinkling stars and said :

> " Shining Star, God's light on high,
>   Look down and prithee see ;
>   Behold me weep and hear me sigh,
>   Then help and pity me.
>   Where my love is canst thou tell ?
>   Thinks he of me ill or well ? "

"You will learn more from the moon," answered the star; "she lives nearer the earth than I, and sees everything that goes on there."

The moon was just rising from her silver bed when Sudolisu called to her:

> "Pearl of the Sky, thou radiant Moon,
>   Thy watch o'er the stars pray leave,
>   Throw thy soft glance o'er the earth ere I swoon,
>   O'ercome by my sorrows I weep and I grieve.
>   I pine for my friend, oh ease thou my heart,
>   And say, am I loved? In his thoughts have I part?"

"Princess," replied the moon, "I know nothing of your friend. But wait a few hours, the sun will have then risen; he knows everything, and will surely be able to tell you."

So the princess kept her eyes fixed upon that part of the sky where the sun first appears, chasing away the darkness like a flock of birds. When he came forth in all his glory she said:

> "Soul of the World, thou deep fountain of life,
>   Eye of all-powerful God,
>   Visit my prison, dark scene of sad strife,
>   Raise up my soul from the sod,
>   With hope that my friend whom I pine for and love
>   May come to my rescue. Say, where does he rove?"

"Sweet Sudolisu," answered the sun, "dry the tears that like pearls roll down your sad and lovely face. Let your troubled heart be at peace, for your friend the prince is now on his way to rescue you. He has recovered the magic ring from the Nether World, and many armies from those countries have assembled to follow him. He is now moving towards Kostey's palace, and intends to punish him. But all this will be of no avail, and Kostey will gain the victory, if the prince does not make use of other means which I am now on my way to provide him with. Farewell; be brave, he whom you love will come to your aid and save you from Kostey and his sorceries; happiness is in store for you both."

The sun then rose upon a distant land where Prince Junak, mounted on a powerful steed and clad in golden armour, assembled his forces to fight against the giant Kostey. Thrice he had dreamt of the beautiful princess shut up in the Sleeping Palace, for the fame of her loveliness had reached him, and he loved without having seen.

"Leave your army where it is," said the sun, "it will not be of the slightest use in fighting against Kostey, he is proof against all weapons. The only way to rescue the princess is to kill him, and there is but one who can tell you how to do it, and that is the witch, old Yaga. I will show you how to find the horse that will carry you straight to her. First take the road to the east, and walk on till you come to a wide plain: there, right in the middle of the plain, are three oaks, and in the centre of these, lying close to the ground, is an iron door with a copper handle. Behind the door is the horse, also an invisible club; both are necessary for the work you have to do. You will learn the rest afterwards. Farewell."

This advice astonished the prince greatly; he hardly knew what to do. After deep reflection he crossed himself, took the magic ring from his finger and cast it into the sea. Instantly the army vanished like mist before the wind, and when not a trace of it was left he took the road to the east. After walking straight on for eight days he reached a large green plain, in the middle of which grew the three oaks, and in the centre of these, close to the ground, was the iron door with the copper handle. Opening the door, he found a winding staircase which led to a second door bound with iron, and shut by means of a huge padlock sixty pounds in weight. At this moment he heard the neighing of a horse, the sound being followed by the opening of eleven other iron doors. There he saw the war-horse which centuries ago had been bewitched by a magician. The prince whistled; the horse immediately bounded towards him, at the same time breaking the twelve iron chains that fastened him to the manger. He was a beautiful creature, strong, light, handsome, full of fire and grace; his eyes flashed lightnings, from his nostrils came flames of fire, his mane was like a cloud of gold, he was certainly a marvel of a horse.

"Prince Junak," said the steed, "I have waited centuries for such a knight as you; here I am, ready to carry you and serve you faithfully. Mount upon my back, and take hold of the invisible club that hangs at the pommel of the saddle. You yourself will not need to use it; give it your orders, it will carry them out and do the fighting itself. Now we will start; may God look after us! Tell me where you wish to go, and you shall be there directly."

The prince quickly told the horse his history, mounted, seized the club, and set off. The creature capered, galloped, flew, and swam in the air higher than the highest forests but lower than the clouds; he crossed mountains, rivers, and precipices; he barely touched the blades of grass in passing over

them, and went so lightly along the roads that he did not raise
one grain of dust.

Towards sunset Junak found himself close to an immense
forest, in the centre of which stood Yaga's house. All around
were oaks and pines hundreds of years old, untouched by the
axe of man. These enormous trees, lit up by the rays of the
setting sun, seemed to look with astonishment at their strange
guest. The silence was absolute; not a bird sang in the
branches, not an insect hummed in the air, not a worm
crawled upon the ground. The only sound was that made
by the horse as he broke through the underwood. Then they
came in sight of a small house supported by a cock's foot,
round which it turned as on a movable pivot. Prince Junak
cried :

> "Turn round, little house, turn round,
>   I want to come inside ;
>   Let thy back to the forest be found,
>   Thy door to me open wide."

The little house turned round, and the prince entering saw
old Yaga, who immediately cried out, "What, Prince Junak!
How have you come here, where no one ever enters?"

"You are a silly old witch, to worry me with questions
instead of making me welcome," said the prince.

At these words old Yaga jumped up and hastened to
attend to his needs. She prepared food and drink, made him
a soft bed where he could sleep comfortably, and then leaving
the house passed the night out of doors. On her return in
the morning the prince related all his adventures and confided
his plans.

"Prince Junak," said she, "you have undertaken a very

difficult task, but your courage will enable you to accomplish it successfully. I will tell you how to kill Kostey, for without that you can do nothing. Now, in the very midst of the ocean lies the Island of Eternal Life. Upon this island is an oak tree, and at the foot of it, hidden in the earth, a coffer bound with iron. A hare is shut up in this coffer, and under her sits a grey duck whose body contains an egg. Within this egg is Kostey's life—if it be broken he dies. Good-bye, Prince Junak, start without loss of time. Your horse will carry you to the island."

Junak mounted his horse, spoke a few words to him, and the brave creature fled through space with the swiftness of an arrow. Leaving the forest and its enormous trees behind, they soon reached the shores of the ocean. Fishermen's nets lay on the beach, and in one of them was a large sea fish who, struggling to free itself, spoke to the prince in a human voice.

"Prince Junak," he said sadly, "free me from my prison; I assure you you will lose nothing by doing me this service."

Junak did what was required of him, and threw the fish back into the water. It plunged and disappeared, but he paid little attention to it, so occupied was he with his own thoughts. In the far distance could be seen the rocks of the Island of Eternal Life, but there seemed no way of reaching it. Leaning on his club he thought and thought, and ever as he thought he grew sadder and sadder.

"What is the matter, Prince Junak? Has anything vexed you?" asked his horse.

"How can I help grieving when, while in sight of the island, I can go no further? How can we cross the sea?"

"Get on my back, prince, I will be your bridge; only take care to hold on tight."

The prince held firmly to its mane, and the horse leapt into the sea. At first they were plunged right beneath the waves, but rising again to the surface swam easily across. The sun was about to set when the prince dismounted on the Island of Eternal Life. He first took off his horse's harness, and leaving him to browse on the green grass, hurried to the top of a distant hill, whence he could see a large oak. Without losing a moment he hastened towards it, seized the tree with both hands, pulled at it with all his might, and after the most violent efforts tore it up by the roots from the place it had filled for centuries. The tree groaned and fell, and the hole in which it had been planted appeared like an immense case. Right at the bottom of this case was a coffer bound with iron. The prince took it up, broke the lock by striking it with a stone, opened it and seized the hare that was trying to make its escape. The grey duck that had lain underneath flew off towards the sea: the prince fired, struck the bird, the latter dropped its egg into the sea, and both were swallowed by the waves. Junak gave a cry of despair and rushed to the beach. At first he could see nothing. After a few minutes there was a slight movement of the waves, while upon the surface swam the fish whose life he had saved. It came towards him, right on to the sand, and dropping the lost egg at his feet, said: "You see, prince, I have not forgotten your kindness, and now I have found it in my power to be of service to you."

Having thus spoken it disappeared in the water. The prince took the egg, mounted his horse, and crossing the sea with his heart full of hope, journeyed towards the island where Princess Sudolisu kept watch over her sleeping subjects in the Enchanted Palace. The latter was surrounded by a wall, and guarded by the Dragon with Twelve Heads. Now these heads went to sleep in turn, six at a time, so it was impossible to take him unawares or to kill him, for that could be done only by his own blows.

On reaching the palace gates Junak sent his invisible club forward to clear the way, whereupon it threw itself upon the dragon, and began to beat all the heads unmercifully. The blows came so thick and fast that the body was soon crushed to pieces. Still the dragon lived and beat the air with its claws. Then it opened its twelve jaws from which darted pointed tongues, but it could not lay hold of the invisible club. At last, tormented on all sides and filled with rage, it buried its sharp claws in its own body and died. The prince then entered the palace gates, and having put his faithful horse in the stables and armed himself with his invisible club, made his way for the tower in which the princess was shut up. On seeing him she cried out, " Prince, I rejoiced to see your victory over the dragon. There is yet a more terrible foe to conquer, and he is my jailor, the cruel Kostey. Beware of him, for if he should kill you, I shall throw myself out of window into the precipice beneath."

" Be comforted, my princess : for in this egg I hold the life or death of Kostey."

Then turning to the invisible club, he said, " Press forward, my invisible club ; strike your best, and rid the earth of this wicked giant."

The club began by breaking down the iron doors, and thus reached Kostey. The giant was soon so crippled with blows that his teeth were smashed, lightnings flashed from his eyes, and he rolled round and round like a pin-cushion. Had he been a man he must have died under such treatment. But he was no man, this master of sorcery. So he managed to get on his feet and look for his tormentor. The blows from the club rained hard upon him all the time, and with such effect that his groans could be heard all over the island. On approaching the window he saw Prince Junak.

"Ah, wretch!" cried the ogre, "it is you, is it, who torments me in this way!" and he prepared to blow upon him with his poisonous breath. But the prince instantly crushed the egg between his hands, the shell broke, the white and yellow mingled and flowed to the ground, and Kostey died.

As the sorcerer breathed his last, the enchantments vanished and the sleeping islanders awoke. The army, once more afoot, advanced with beating drums to the palace, and everything fell into its accustomed place. As soon as Princess Sudolisu was freed from her prison she held out her white hand to her deliverer, and thanking him in the most touching words, led him to the throne and placed him at her side. The twelve maids of honour having chosen young and brave warriors, ranged themselves with their lovers round the queen. Then the doors were thrown open, and the priests in their robes entered, bearing a golden tray of wedding rings. Thereupon the marriage ceremony was gone through, and the lovers united in God's name.

After the wedding there were feasting and music and
dancing, as is usual on such occasions, and they all enjoyed
themselves. It makes one glad to think how happy they
were, and what a glorious time they had after their misfortunes.

THE PRINCE WITH
THE GOLDEN HAND

THE PRINCE WITH THE GOLDEN HAND

THERE once lived a king and queen who had an only daughter. And the beauty of this princess surpassed everything seen or heard of. Her forehead was brilliant as the moon, her lips like the rose, her complexion had the delicacy of the lily, and her breath the sweetness of jessamine. Her hair was golden, and in her voice and glance there was something so enchanting that none could help listening to her or looking at her.

The princess lived for seventeen years in her own rooms, rejoicing the heart of her parents, teachers, and servants. No one else ever saw her, for the sons of the king and all other princes were forbidden to enter her rooms. She never went anywhere, never looked upon the outside world, and never breathed the outer air, but she was perfectly happy.

When she was eighteen it happened, either by chance or by the will of fate, that she heard the cry of the cuckoo. This sound made her strangely uneasy; her golden head drooped, and covering her eyes with her hands, she fell into thought so deep as not to hear her mother enter. The queen looked at her anxiously, and after comforting her went to tell the king about it.

For many years past the sons of kings and neighbouring princes had, either personally or by their ambassadors, presented themselves at court to ask the king for the hand of his daughter in marriage. But he had always bidden them wait until another time. Now, after a long consultation with the queen, he sent messengers to foreign courts and elsewhere to proclaim that the princess, in accordance with the wishes of her parents, was about to choose a husband, and that the man of her choice would also have the right of succession to the throne.

When the princess heard of this decision her joy was very great, and for days she would dream about it. Then she looked out into the garden through the golden lattice of her window, and longed with an irresistible longing to walk in the open air upon the smooth lawn. With great difficulty she at last persuaded her governesses to allow her to do so, they agreeing on condition that she should keep with them. So the crystal doors were thrown open, the oaken gates that shut in the orchard turned on their hinges, and the princess found herself on the green grass. She ran about, picking the sweet-scented flowers and chasing the many-coloured butterflies. But she could not have been a very prudent maiden, for she wandered away from her governesses, with her face uncovered.

Just at that moment a raging hurricane, such as had never been seen or heard before, passed by and fell upon the garden. It roared and whistled round and round, then seizing the princess carried her far away. The terrified governesses wrung their hands, and were for a time speechless with grief. At last they rushed into the palace, and throwing themselves on their knees before the king and queen, told them with sobs and tears what had happened. They were overwhelmed with sorrow and knew not what to do.

By this time quite a crowd of princes had arrived at the palace, and seeing the king in such bitter grief, inquired the reason of it.

"Sorrow has touched my white hairs," said the king. "The hurricane has carried off my dearly beloved child, the sweet Princess with the Golden Hair, and I know not where it has taken her. Whoever finds this out, and brings her back to me, shall have her for his wife, and with her half my kingdom for a wedding present, and the remainder of my wealth and titles after my death."

After hearing these words, princes and knights mounted their horses and set off to search throughout the world for

the beautiful Princess with the Golden Hair, who had been
carried away by Vikher.

Now among the seekers were two brothers, sons of a king,
and they travelled together through many countries asking
for news of the princess, but no one knew anything about
her.   But they continued their search, and at the end of two
years arrived in a country that lies in the centre of the earth,
and has summer and winter at the same time.

The princes determined to find out whether this was the
place where the hurricane had hidden the Princess with the
Golden Hair.   So they began to ascend one of the mountains
on foot, leaving their horses behind them to feed on the grass.
On reaching the top, they came in sight of a silver palace
supported on a cock's foot, while at one of the windows the
sun's rays shone upon a head of golden hair; surely it could
only belong to the princess.   Suddenly the north wind blew
so violently, and the cold became so intense, that the leaves
of the trees withered and the breath froze.   The two princes
tried to keep their footing, and battled manfully against the
storm, but they were overcome by its fierceness and fell
together, frozen to death.

Their broken-hearted parents waited for them in vain.
Masses were said, charities distributed, and prayers sent up
to God to pity them in their sorrow.

One day when the queen, the mother of the princes, was
giving a poor old man some money she said to him, "My good
old friend, pray God to guard our sons and soon bring them
back in good health."

"Ah, noble lady," answered he, "that prayer would be
useless.   Everlasting rest is all one may ask for the dead,

but in return for the love you have shown and the money you have given the poor and needy, I am charged with this message—that God has taken pity on your sorrow, and that ere long you will be the mother of a son, the like of whom has never yet been seen."

The old man, having spoken thus, vanished.

The queen, whose tears were falling, felt a strange joy enter her heart and a feeling of happiness steal over her, as she went to the king and repeated the old man's words. And so it came to pass, for a week or two later God sent her a son, and he was in no way like an ordinary child. His eyes resembled those of a falcon, and his eyebrows the sable's fur. His right hand was of pure gold, and his manner and appearance were so full of an indescribable majesty, that he was looked upon by every one with a feeling of awe.

His growth, too, was not like that of other children. When but three days old, he stepped out of his swaddling-clothes and left his cradle. And he was so strong that when his parents entered the room he ran towards them, crying out, "Good morning, dear parents, why are you so sad? Are you not happy at the sight of me?"

"We are indeed happy, dear child, and we thank God for having sent us you in our great grief. But we cannot forget your two brothers; they were so handsome and brave, and worthy of a great destiny. And our sadness is increased when we remember that, instead of resting in their own country in the tomb of their forefathers, they sleep in an unknown land, perhaps without burial. Alas! it is three years since we had news of them."

At these words the child's tears fell, and he embraced his

parents and said, "Weep no more, dear parents, you shall soon be comforted : for before next spring I shall be a strong young man, and will look for my brothers all over the world. And I will bring them back to you, if not alive, yet dead : ay, though I have to seek them in the very centre of the earth."

At these words and at that which followed the king and queen were amazed. For the strange child, guided as it were by an invisible hand, rushed into the garden, and in spite of the cold, for it was not yet daylight, bathed in the early dew. When the sun had risen he threw himself down near a little wood on the fine sand, rubbed and rolled himself in it, and returned home, no longer a child but a youth.

It was pleasant to the king to see his son thrive in this way, and indeed the young prince was the handsomest in the whole land. He grew from hour to hour. At the end of a month he could wield a sword, in two months he rode on horseback, in three months he had grown a beautiful moustache of pure gold. Then he put on a helmet, and presenting himself before the king and queen, said : "My much honoured parents, your son asks your blessing. I am no longer a child, and now go to seek my brothers. In order to find them I will, if necessary, go to the furthest ends of the world."

"Ah, do not venture. Stay rather with us, dear son, you are still too young to be exposed to the risks of such an undertaking."

"Adventures have no terrors for me," replied the young hero, "I trust in God. Why should I for a moment hesitate to face these dangers? Whatever Destiny has in store for us will happen, whatever we may do to try to prevent it."

So they agreed to let him go. Weeping they bade him farewell, blessing him and the road he was to travel.

A pleasant tale is soon told, but events do not pass so quickly.

The young prince crossed deep rivers and climbed high mountains, till he came to a dark forest. In the distance he saw a cottage supported on a cock's foot, and standing in the midst of a field full of poppies. As he made his ways towards it he was suddenly seized by an overpowering longing to sleep, but he urged on his horse, and breaking off the poppy heads as he galloped through the field, came up close to the house. Then he called out :

> " Little cot, turn around, on thy foot turn thou free ;
> To the forest set thy back, let thy door be wide to me."

The cottage turned round with a great creaking noise, the door facing the prince. He entered, and found an old woman with thin white hair and a face covered with wrinkles, truly frightful to look upon. She was sitting at a table, her head resting on her hands, her eyes fixed on the ceiling, lost in deep thought. Near her were two beautiful girls, their complexions like lilies and roses, and in every way sweet to the eye.

" Ah, how do you do, Prince with Moustache of Gold, Hero with the Golden Fist ? " said old Yaga ; " what has brought you here ? "

Having told her the object of his journey, she replied, " Your elder brothers perished on the mountain that touches the clouds, while in search of the Princess with the Golden Hair, who was carried off by Vikher, the hurricane."

"And how is this thief Vikher to be got at?" asked the prince.

"Ah, my dear child, he would swallow you like a fly. It is now a hundred years since I went outside this cottage, for fear Vikher should seize me and carry me off to his palace near the sky."

"I am not afraid of his carrying me off, I am not handsome enough for that; and he will not swallow me either, for my golden hand can smash anything."

"Then if you are not afraid, my dove, I will help you to the best of my power. But give me your word of honour that you will bring me some of the Water of Youth, for it restores even to the most aged the beauty and freshness of youth."

"I give you my word of honour that I will bring you some."

"This then is what you must do. I will give you a pin-cushion for a guide; this you throw in front of you, and follow whithersoever it goes. It will lead you to the mountain that touches the clouds, and which is guarded in Vikher's absence by his father and mother, the northern blast and the south wind. On no account lose sight of the pin-cushion. If attacked by the father, the northern blast, and suddenly seized with cold, then put on this heat-giving hood: if overpowered by burning heat of the south wind, then drink from this cooling flagon. Thus by means of the pin-cushion, the hood, and the flagon, you will reach the top of the mountain where the Princess with the Golden Hair is imprisoned. Deal with Vikher as you will, only remember to bring me some of the Water of Youth."

Our young hero took the heat-giving hood, the cooling

flagon, and the pin-cushion, and, after bidding farewell to old Yaga and her two pretty daughters, mounted his steed and rode off, following the pin-cushion, which rolled before him at a great rate.

Now a beautiful story is soon told, but the events of which it consists do not in real life take place so rapidly.

When the prince had travelled through two kingdoms, he came to a land in which lay a very beautiful valley that stretched into the far distance, and above it towered the mountain that touches the sky. The summit was so high above the earth you might almost fancy it reached the moon.

The prince dismounted, left his horse to graze, and having crossed himself began to follow the pin-cushion up steep and rocky paths. When he had got half-way there the north wind began to blow, and the cold was so intense that the wood of the trees split up and the breath froze: he felt chilled to the heart. But he quickly put on the heat-giving hood, and cried :

> "O Heat-Giving Hood, see I fly now to thee,
>   Lend me quickly thine aid ;
> O hasten to warm ere the cold has killed me,
>   With thee I'm not afraid."

The northern blast blew with redoubled fury, but to no purpose. For the prince was so hot that he streamed with perspiration, and indeed was obliged to unbutton his coat and fan himself.

Here the pin-cushion stopped upon a small snow-covered mound. The prince cleared away the snow, beneath which lay the frozen bodies of two young men, and he knew them to be those of his lost brothers. Having knelt beside them and prayed he turned to follow the pin-cushion, which had already started, and was rolling ever higher and higher. On reaching the top of the mountain he saw a silver palace supported on a cock's foot, and at one of the windows, shining in the sun's rays, a head of golden hair which could belong to no one but the princess. Suddenly a hot wind began to blow from the south, and the heat became so intense that leaves withered and dropped from the trees, the grass dried up, and large cracks appeared in several places of the earth's surface. Thirst, heat, and weariness began to tell upon the young prince, so he took the cooling flagon from his pocket and cried:

> "Flagon, bring me quick relief
> From this parching heat ;
> In thy draught I have belief,
> Coolness it will mete."

After drinking deeply he felt stronger than ever, and so continued to ascend. Not only was he relieved from the great heat, but was even obliged to button up his coat to keep himself warm.

The pin-cushion still led the way, ever climbing higher and higher, while the prince followed close behind. After crossing the region of clouds they came to the topmost peak of the mountain. Here the prince came close to the palace, which can only be likened to a dream of perfect beauty. It was supported on a cock's foot, and was built entirely of silver, except for its steel gates and roof of solid gold. Before the entrance was a deep precipice over which none but the birds could pass. As the prince gazed upon the splendid building the princess leaned out of one of the windows, and seeing him

light shone from her sparkling eyes, her lovely hair floated in the wind, and the scent of her sweet breath filled the air. The prince sprang forward and cried out:

“Silver Palace, oh turn, on thy foot turn thou free,
  To the steep rocks thy back, but thy doors wide to me.”

At these words it revolved creaking, the doorway facing the prince. As he entered it returned to its original position. The prince went through the palace till he came to a room bright as the sun itself, and the walls, floor, and ceiling of which consisted of mirrors. He was filled with wonder, for instead of one princess he saw twelve, all equally beautiful, with the same graceful movements and golden hair. But eleven were only reflections of the one real princess. She gave a cry of joy on seeing him, and running to meet him, said: “Ah, noble sir, you look like a delivering angel. Surely you bring me good news. From what family, city, or country have you come? Perhaps my dear father and mother sent you in search of me?”

“No one has sent me, I have come of my own free will to rescue you and restore you to your parents.”

When he had told her all that had passed she said, “Your devotion, prince, is very great; may God bless your attempt. But Vikher the hurricane is unconquerable, so, if life be dear to you, fly. Leave this place before his return, which I expect every minute; he will kill you with one glance of his eyes.”

“If I should not succeed in saving you, sweet princess, life can be no longer dear to me. But I am full of hope, and I beg you first to give me some of the Strength-Giving

Water from the Heroic Well, for this is drunk by the hurricane."

The princess drew a bucketful of water, which the young man emptied at one draught and then asked for another. This astonished her somewhat, but she gave it him, and when he had drunk it he said, "Allow me, princess, to sit down for a moment to take breath."

She gave him an iron chair, but directly he sat down it broke into a thousand pieces. She then brought him the chair used by Vikher himself, but although it was made of the strongest steel, it bent and creaked beneath the prince's weight.

"Now you see," said he, "that I have grown heavier than your unconquerable hurricane: so take courage, with God's help and your good wishes I shall overcome him. In the meantime tell me how you pass your time here."

"Alas! in bitter tears and sad reflections. My only consolation is that I have been able to keep my persecutor at a distance, for he vainly implores me to marry him. Two years have now passed away, and yet none of his efforts to win my consent have been successful. Last time he went away he told me that if on his return he had not guessed the riddles I set him (the correct explanation of these being the condition I have made for his marrying me), he would set them aside, and marry me in spite of my objections."

"Ah, then I am just in time. I will be the priest on that occasion, and give him Death for a bride."

At that moment a horrible whistling was heard.

"Be on your guard, prince," cried she, "here comes the hurricane."

The palace spun rapidly round, fearful sounds filled the building, thousands of ravens and birds of ill omen croaked loudly and flapped their wings, and all the doors opened with a tremendous noise.

Vikher, mounted on his winged horse that breathed fire, leapt into the mirrored room, then stopped amazed at the sight before him. He was indeed the hurricane, with the body of a giant and the head of a dragon, and as he gazed his horse pranced and beat his wings.

"What is your business here, stranger?" he shouted : and the sound of his voice was like unto a lion's roar.

"I am your enemy, and I want your blood," replied the prince calmly.

"Your boldness amuses me. At the same time, if you do not depart at once I will take you in my left hand and crush every bone in your body with my right."

"Try, if you dare, woman-stealer," he answered.

Vikher roared, breathing fire in his rage, and with his mouth wide open threw himself upon the prince, intending to swallow him. But the latter stepped lightly aside, and putting his golden hand down his enemy's throat, seized him by the tongue and dashed him against the wall with such force that the monster bounded against it like a ball, and died within a few moments, shedding torrents of blood.

The prince then drew from different springs the water that *restores*, that *revives*, and that *makes young*, and taking the unconscious girl in his arms he led the winged horse to the door and said :

> "Silver Palace, oh turn, on thy foot turn thou free,
>   To the steep rocks thy back, the courtyard may I see."

Whereupon the palace creaked round on the cock's foot, and the door opened on the courtyard. Mounting the horse he placed the princess before him, for she had by this time recovered from her swoon, and cried :

> " Fiery Horse with strength of wing,
>   I am now your lord ;
>   Do my will in everything,
>   Be your law my word.
>   Where I point there you must go
>   At once, at once. The way you know."

And he pointed to the place where his brothers lay frozen in death. The horse rose, pranced, beat the air with his wings, then, lifting himself high in the air, came down gently where the two princes were lying. The Prince with the Golden Hand sprinkled their bodies with the Life-Restoring Water, and instantly the pallor of death disappeared, leaving in its place the natural colour. He then sprinkled them with the Water that Revives, after which they opened their eyes, got up, and looking round said, " How well we have slept : but what has happened? And how is it we see the lovely princess we sought in the society of a young man, a perfect stranger to us ? "

The Prince with the Golden Hand explained everything, embraced his brothers tenderly, and taking them with him on his horse, showed the latter that he wished to go in the direction of Yaga's cottage. The horse rose up, pranced, lifted himself in the air, then, beating his wings far above the highest forests, descended close by the cottage. The prince said :

> " Little cot, turn around, on thy foot turn thou free,
>   To the forest thy back, but thy door wide to me."

The cottage began to creak without delay, and turned round with the floor facing the travellers. Old Yaga was on the look-out, and came to meet them. As soon as she got the Water of Youth she sprinkled herself with it, and instantly everything about her that was old and ugly became young and charming. So pleased was she to be young again that she kissed the prince's hands and said, "Ask of me anything you like, I will refuse you nothing."

At that moment her two beautiful young daughters happened to look out of the window, upon which the two elder princes, who were admiring them, said, "Will you give us your daughters for wives?"

"That I will, with pleasure," said she, and beckoned them to her. Then curtseying to her future sons-in-law, she laughed merrily and vanished. They placed their brides before them on the same horse, while the Prince with the Golden Hand, pointing to where he wished to go, said :

> " Fiery Horse with strength of wing,
>   I am now your lord ;
>   Do my will in everything,
>   Be your law my word.
>   Where I point there you must go
>   At once, at once. The way you know."

The horse rose up, pranced, flapped his wings, and flew far above the forest. An hour or two later he descended before the palace of the Golden-Haired Princess's parents. When the king and queen saw their only daughter who had so long been lost to them, they ran to meet her with exclamations of joy and kissed her gratefully and lovingly, at the same

time thanking the prince who had restored her to them.　And
when they heard the story of his adventures they said: "You,
Prince with the Golden Hand, shall receive our beloved
daughter in marriage, with the half of our kingdom, and the
right of succession to the remainder after us.　Let us, too,
add to the joy of this day by celebrating the weddings of your
two brothers."

The Princess with the Golden Hair kissed her father
lovingly and said, "My much honoured and noble sire and
lord, the prince my bridegroom knows of the vow I made
when carried off by the hurricane, that I would only give my
hand to him who could answer aright my six enigmas: it
would be impossible for the Princess with the Golden Hair
to break her word."

The king was silent, but the prince said, "Speak, sweet
princess, I am listening."

"This is my first riddle: 'Two of my extremities form a
sharp point, the two others a ring, in my centre is a screw.'"

"A pair of scissors," answered he.

"Well guessed.　This is the second: 'I make the round
of the table on only one foot, but if I am wounded the evil
is beyond repair.'"

"A glass of wine."

"Right.　This is the third: 'I have no tongue, and yet I
answer faithfully; I am not seen, yet every one hears me.'"

"An echo."

"True.　This is the fourth: 'Fire cannot light me; brush
cannot sweep me; no painter can paint me; no hiding-place
secure me.'"

"Sunshine."

"'The very thing. This is the fifth: 'I existed before the creation of Adam. I am always changing in succession the two colours of my dress. Thousands of years have gone by, but I have remained unaltered both in colour and form.'"

"It must be time, including day and night."

"You have succeeded in guessing the five most difficult, the last is the easiest of all. 'By day a ring, by night a serpent; he who guesses this shall be my bridegroom.'"

"It is a girdle."

"Now they are all guessed," said she, and gave her hand to the young prince.

They knelt before the king and queen to receive their blessing. The three weddings were celebrated that same evening, and a messenger mounted the winged horse to carry the good news to the parents of the young princes and to bring them back as guests. Meanwhile a magnificent feast was prepared, and invitations were sent to all their friends and acquaintances. And from that evening until the next morning they ceased not to feast and drink and dance. I too was a guest, and feasted with the rest; but though I ate and drank, the wine only ran down my beard, and my throat remained dry.

IMPERISHABLE

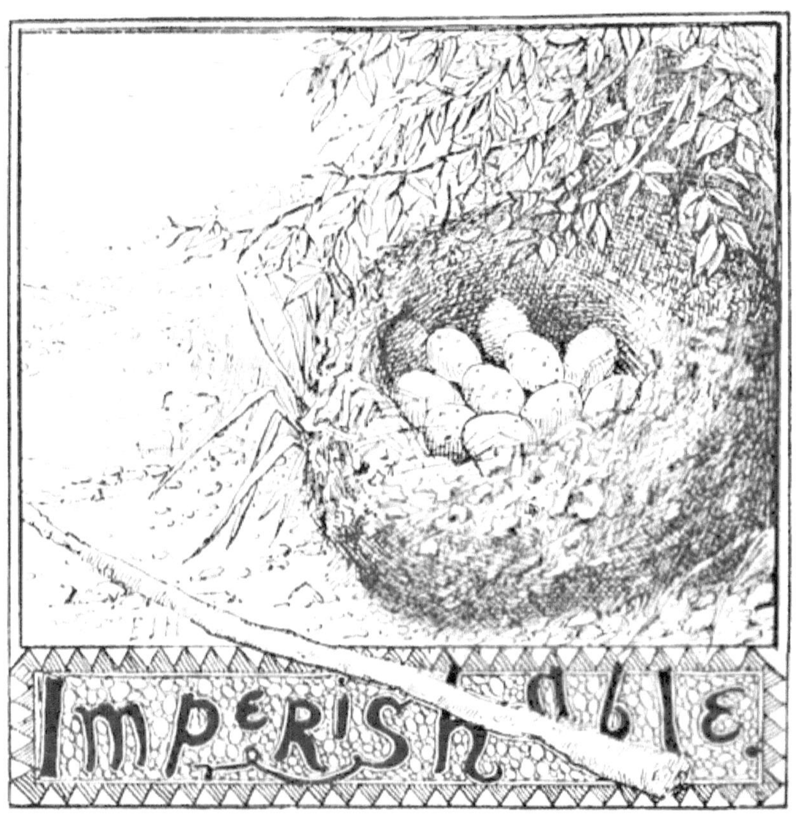

ONCE upon a time, ever so many years ago, there lived a little old man and a little old woman. Very old indeed were they, for they had lived nearly a hundred years. But they took neither joy nor pleasure in anything, and this because they had no children. They were now about to keep the seventy-fifth anniversary of their wedding day, known as the Diamond Wedding, but no guests were invited to share their simple feast.

As they sat side by side they went over in memory the years of their long life, and as they did so they felt sure that it was to punish them for their sins that God had denied them the sweet happiness of having children about them, and as they thought their tears fell fast. At that moment some one knocked.

"Who is there?" cried the old woman, and ran to open the door. There stood a little old man leaning on a stick, and white as a dove.

"What do you want?" asked the old woman.

"Charity," answered he.

The good old woman was kind-hearted, and she cut her last loaf in two, giving one half to the beggar, who said, "I see you have been weeping, good wife, and I know the reason of your tears; but cheer up, by God's grace you shall be comforted. Though poor and childless to-day, to-morrow you shall have family and fortune."

When the old woman heard this she was overjoyed, and fetching her husband they both went to the door to invite the old man in. But he was gone, and though they searched for him in every direction they found nothing but his stick lying on the ground. For it was not a poor old beggar, but an angel of God who had knocked. Our good friends did not know this, so they picked up the stick and hurried off to find the old man, with the purpose of returning it. But it seemed as if the stick, like its master, were endowed with some marvellous power, for whenever the old man or the old woman tried to pick it up it slipped out of their hands and rolled along the ground. Thus they followed it into a forest, and at the foot of a shrub which stood close by a stream it disappeared. They hunted all round the shrub thinking to find the stick there, but instead of the stick they came upon a bird's nest containing twelve eggs, and from the shape of the shells it seemed as if the young ones were ready to come forth.

"Pick up the eggs," said the old man, "they will make us an omelette for our wedding feast."

The old woman grumbled a little, but she took the nest and carried it home in the skirt of her gown. Fancy their astonishment when at the end of twelve hours there came out, not unfledged birdlings, but twelve pretty little boys. Then the shells broke into tiny fragments which were changed into as many gold pieces. Thus, as had been foretold, the old man and his wife found both family and fortune.

Now these twelve boys were most extraordinary children. Directly they came out of the shells they seemed to be at least three months old, such a noise did they make, crying and kicking about. The youngest of all was a very big baby with black eyes, red cheeks, and curly hair, and so lively and active that the old woman could hardly keep him in his cradle at all. In twelve hours' time the children seemed to be a year old, and could walk about and eat anything.

Then the old woman made up her mind that they should be baptized, and thereupon sent her husband to fetch priest and organist without delay; and the diamond wedding was celebrated at the same time as the christening. For a short time their joy was clouded over by the disappearance of the youngest boy, who was also the best-looking, and his parents' favourite. They had begun to weep and mourn for him as if he were lost, when suddenly he was seen to come from out of the sleeves of the priest's cassock, and was heard to speak these words: "Never fear, dear parents, your beloved son will not perish."

The old woman kissed him fondly and handed him to his godfather, who presented him to the priest. So they had named him *Niezguinek*, that is, *Imperishable*. The twelve boys went on growing at the rate of six weeks every hour, and at the end of two years were fine strong young men. Niezguinek, especially, was of extraordinary size and strength. The good old people lived happily and peacefully at home while their sons worked in the fields. On one occasion the latter went ploughing; and while the eleven eldest used the ordinary plough and team of oxen, Niezguinek made his own plough, and it had twelve ploughshares and twelve handles, and to it were harnessed twelve team of the strongest working oxen. The others laughed at him, but he did not mind, and turned up as much ground as his eleven brothers together.

Another time when they went haymaking and his brothers used the ordinary scythes, he carried one with twelve blades, and managed it so cleverly, in spite of the jests of his companions, that he cut as much grass as all of them together. And again, when they went to turn over the hay, Niezguinek used a rake with twelve teeth, and so cleared twelve plots of ground with every stroke. His haycock, too, was as large as a hill in comparison with those of his brothers. Now, the day after the making of the haycocks the old man and his wife happened to be in the fields, and they noticed that one haycock had disappeared; so thinking wild horses had made off with it, they advised their sons to take turns in watching the place.

The eldest took his turn first, but after having watched all night fell asleep towards morning, when he awoke to find another haycock missing. The second son was not more fortunate in preventing the disappearance of the hay, while the others succeeded no better; in fact, of all the twelve haycocks, there only remained the largest, Niezguinek's, and even that had been meddled with.

When it was the youngest's turn to watch, he went to the village blacksmith and got him to make an iron club weighing two hundred and sixty pounds; so heavy was it that the blacksmith and his assistants could hardly turn it on the anvil. In order to test it, Niezguinek whirled it round his head and threw it up in the air, and when it had nearly reached the ground he caught it on his knee, upon which it was smashed to atoms. He then ordered another weighing four hundred and eighty pounds, and this the blacksmith and his men could not even move. Niezguinek had helped them to make it, and when finished he tested it in the same manner as the first. Finding it did not break he kept it, and had in addition a noose plaited with twelve strong ropes. Towards nightfall he went to the field, crouched down behind his haycock, crossed himself, and waited to see what would happen. At midnight there was a tremendous noise which seemed to come from the east, while in that direction appeared a bright light. Then a white mare, with twelve colts as white as herself, trotted up to the haycock and began to eat it. Niezguinek came out of his hiding-place, and throwing the noose over the mare's neck, jumped on her back and struck her with his heavy club. The terrified creature gave the signal to the colts to escape, but she herself, hindered by the noose, out of breath, and wounded by the club, could not follow, but sank down on the earth saying, "Do not choke me, Niezguinek."

He marvelled to hear her speak human language, and loosened the noose. When she had taken breath she said, "Knight, if you give me my liberty you shall never repent it. My husband, the Dappled Horse with Golden Mane, will cruelly revenge himself upon you when he knows I am your prisoner; his strength and swiftness are so great you could not escape him. In exchange for my freedom I will give you my twelve colts, who will serve you and your brothers faithfully."

On hearing their mother neigh the colts returned and stood with bent heads before the young man, who released the mare, and led them home. The brothers were delighted to see Niezguinek return with twelve beautiful white horses, and each took the one that pleased his fancy most, while the thinnest and weakest-looking was left for the youngest.

The old couple were happy in the thought that their son was brave as well as strong. One day it occurred to the old woman that she would like to see them all married, and to have the house merry with her daughters-in-law and their children. So she called upon her gossips and friends to talk the matter over, and finally persuaded her husband to be of the same opinion. He called his sons around him and addressed them thus: "Listen to me, my sons: in a certain country lives a celebrated witch known as old Yaga. She is lame, and travels about in an oaken trough. She supports herself on iron crutches, and when she goes abroad carefully

removes all traces of her steps with a broom. This old witch has twelve beautiful daughters who have large dowries: do your best to win them for your wives. Do not return without bringing them with you."

Both parents blessed their sons, who, mounting their horses, were soon out of sight. All but Niezguinek, who, left alone, went to the stable and began to shed tears.

"Why do you weep?" asked his horse.

"Don't you think I have good reason?" replied he. "Here I have to go a long long way in search of a wife, and you, my friend, are so thin and weak that were I to depend upon your strength I should never be able to join my brothers."

"Do not despair, Niezguinek," said the horse, "not only will you overtake your brothers, but you will leave them far behind. I am the son of the Dappled Horse with the Golden Mane, and if you will do exactly as I tell you I shall be given the same power as he. You must kill me and bury me under a layer of earth and manure, then sow some wheat over me, and when the corn is ripe it must be gathered and some of it placed near my body."

Niezguinek threw his arms round his horse's neck and kissed him fondly, then led him into a yard and killed him with one blow of his club. The horse staggered a moment and then fell dead. His master covered him with a layer of manure and earth, upon which he sowed wheat, as had been directed. It was immediately watered by a gentle rain, and warmed by the heat of the sun's rays. The corn took root and ripened so quickly that on the twelfth day Niezguinek set to work to cut, thresh, and winnow it. So abundant was it that he was

Q

able to give eleven measures to his parents, and keeping one
for himself, spread it before his horse's bones. In a very
short time the horse moved his head, sniffed the air, and began
to devour the wheat. As soon as it was finished he sprang
up, and was so full of life that he wanted to jump over the
fence in one bound: but Niezguinek held him by the mane,
and getting lightly on his back, said: " Halt there, my spirited
steed, I do not want others to have the benefit of all the
trouble I have had with you. Carry me to old Yaga's house."

He was of a truth a most magnificent horse, big and strong,
with eyes that flashed like lightning. He leapt up into the
air as high as the clouds, and the next moment descended
in the middle of a field, saying to his master: " As we have
first to see old Yaga, from whom we are still a great way
off, we can stop here for a short time: take food and rest,
I will do the same. Your brothers will be obliged to pass
us, for we are a good way in front of them. When they
come you can go on together to visit the old witch: remember, though it is difficult to get into her house, it is
much more difficult still to get out. But if you would be
perfectly safe, take from under my saddle a brush, a scarf,
and a handkerchief. They will be of use in helping you to
escape ; for when you unroll the scarf, a river will flow between
you and your enemy; if you shake the brush it will become
a thick forest; and by waving the handkerchief it will be
changed into a lake. After you have been received into
Yaga's house, and your brothers have stabled their horses
and gone to bed, I will tell you how to act."

For twelve days Niezguinek and his horse rested and
gained strength, and at the end of the time the eleven

brothers came up. They wondered greatly to see the youngest, and said, "Where on earth did you come from? And whose horse is that?"

"I have come from home. The horse is the same I chose at first. We have been waiting here twelve days; let us go on together now."

Within a short time they came to a house surrounded by a high oaken paling, at the gate of which they knocked. Old Yaga peeped out through a chink in the fence and cried, "Who are you? What do you want?"

"We are twelve brothers come to ask the twelve daughters of Yaga in marriage. If she is willing to be our mother-in-law, let her open the door."

The door was opened and Yaga appeared. She was a frightful-looking creature, old as the hills; and being one of those monsters who feed on human flesh, the unfortunate wretches who once entered her house never came out again. She had a lame leg, and because of this she leaned on a great iron crutch, and when she went out removed all traces of her steps with a broom.

She received the young travellers very graciously, shut the gate of the courtyard behind them, and led them into the house. Niezguinek's brothers dismounted, and taking their horses to the stables, tied them up to rings made of silver; the youngest fastened his to a copper ring. The old witch served her guests with a good supper, and gave them wine and hydromel to drink. Then she made up twelve beds on the right side of the room for the travellers, and on the left side twelve beds for her daughters.

All were soon asleep except Niezguinek. He had been

warned beforehand by his horse of the danger that threatened them, and now he got up quietly and changed the positions of the twenty-four beds, so that the brothers lay to the left side of the room, and Yaga's daughters to the right. At midnight, old Yaga cried out in a hoarse voice, "Guzla, play. Sword, strike."

Then were heard strains of sweet music, to which the old woman beat time from her oaken trough. At the same moment a slender sword descended into the room, and passing over to the beds on the right, cut off the heads of the girls one by one: after which it danced about and flashed in the darkness.

When the dawn broke the guzla ceased playing, the sword disappeared, and silence reigned. Then Niezguinek softly aroused his brothers, and they all went out without making any noise. Each mounted his horse, and when they had broken open the yard gate they made their escape at full speed. Old Yaga, thinking she heard footsteps, got up and ran into the room where her daughters lay dead. At the dreadful sight she gnashed her teeth, barked like a dog, tore out her hair by handfuls, and seating herself in her trough as in a car, set off after the fugitives. She had nearly reached them, and was already stretching out her hand to seize them, when Niezguinek unrolled his magic scarf, and instantly a deep river flowed between her and the horsemen. Not being able to cross it she stopped on the banks, and howling savagely began to drink it up.

"Before you have swallowed all that river you will burst, you wicked old witch," cried Niezguinek. Then he rejoined his brothers.

But the old woman drank all the water, crossed the bed of the river in her trough, and soon came near the young people. Niezguinek shook his handkerchief, and a lake immediately spread out between them. So she was again obliged to stop, and shrieking with rage began to drink up the water.

"Before you have drunk that lake dry you will have burst yourself," said Niezguinek, and rode after his brothers.

The old vixen drank up part of the water, and turning the remainder into a thick fog, hastened along in her trough. She was once more close upon the young men when Niezguinek, without a moment's delay, seized his brush, and as he waved it in the air a thick forest rose between them. For a time the witch was at a loss to know what to do. On one side she saw Niezguinek and his brothers rapidly disappearing, while she stood on the other hindered by the branches and torn by the thorns of the thick bushes, unable either to advance or retreat. Foaming with rage, with fire flashing from her eyes, she struck right and left with her crutches, crashing trees on all sides, but before she could clear a way those she was in pursuit of had got more than a hundred miles ahead.

So she was forced to give up, and grinding her teeth, howling, and tearing out her hair, she threw after the fugitives such flaming glances from her eyes that she set the forest on fire, and taking the road home was soon lost to sight.

The travellers, seeing the flames, guessed what had happened, and thanked God for having preserved them from such great dangers. They continued their journey, and by eventide arrived at the top of a steep hill. There they saw a town besieged by foreign troops, who had already destroyed the outer part, and only awaited daylight to take it by storm.

The twelve brothers kept out of sight behind the enemy; and when they had rested and turned out their horses to graze all went to sleep except Niezguinek, who kept watch without closing an eye. When everything was perfectly still he got up, and calling his horse, said, " Listen; yonder in that tent sleeps the king of this besieging army, and he dreams of the victory he hopes for on the morrow: how could we send all the soldiers to sleep and get possession of his person?"

The horse replied, "You will find some dried leaves of the herb of Sleep in the pocket of the saddle. Mount upon my back and hover round the camp, spreading fragments of the plant. That will cause all the soldiers to fall into a sound sleep, after which you can carry out your plans."

Niezguinek mounted his horse, pronouncing these magic words :

> " Marvel of strength and of beauty so white,
> Horse of my heart, let us go ;
> Rise in the air, like a bird take thy flight,
> Haste to the camp of the foe."

The horse glanced upwards as if he saw some one beckoning to him from the clouds, then rose rapidly as a bird on the wing and hovered over the camp. Niezguinek took handfuls of the herb of Sleep from the saddle-pockets and sprinkled it all about. Upon which all in the camp, including the sentinels, fell at once into a heavy sleep. Niezguinek alighted, entered the tent, and carried off the sleeping king without any difficulty. He then returned to his brothers, unharnessed his horse and lay down to rest, placing the royal prisoner near him. His majesty slept on as if nothing unusual had taken place.

At daybreak the soldiers of the besieging army awoke, and not being able to find their king, were seized with such a panic of terror that they retreated in great disorder. The ruler of the besieged city would not at first believe that the enemy had really disappeared, and indeed went himself to see if it was true: of a truth there remained nothing of the enemy's camp but a few deserted tents whitening on the plain. At that moment Niezguinek came up with his brothers, and said, "Sire, the enemy has fled, and we were unable to detain them, but here is their king whom we have made prisoner, and whom I deliver up to you."

The ruler replied, "I see, indeed, that you are a brave man among brave men, and I will reward you. This royal prisoner is worth a large ransom to me; so speak,—what would you like me to do for you?"

"I should wish, sire, that my brothers and I might enter the service of your majesty."

"I am quite willing," answered the king. Then, having placed his prisoner in charge of his guards, he made Niezguinek general, and placed him at the head of a division of his army; the eleven brothers were given the rank of officers.

When Niezguinek appeared in uniform, and with sabre in hand mounted his splendid charger, he looked so handsome and conducted the manœuvres so well that he surpassed all the other chiefs in the country, thus causing much jealousy, even among his own brothers, for they were vexed that the youngest should outshine them, and so determined to ruin him.

In order to accomplish this they imitated his handwriting, and placed such a note before the king's door while

Niezguinek was engaged elsewhere. When the king went out he found the letter, and calling Niezguinek to him, said, "I should very much like to have the phonic guzla you mention in your letter."

"But, sire, I have not written anything about a guzla," said he.

"Read the note then. Is it not in your handwriting?"

Niezguinek read:

"In a certain country, within the house of old Yaga, is a marvellous guzla: if the king wish I will fetch it for him.

"(Signed)   NIEZGUINEK."

"It is true," said he, "that this writing resembles mine, but it is a forgery, for I never wrote it."

"Never mind," said the king, "as you were able to take my enemy prisoner you will certainly be able to succeed in getting old Yaga's guzla: go then, and do not return without it, or you will be executed."

Niezguinek bowed and went out. He went straight to the stable, where he found his charger looking very sad and thin, his head drooping before the trough, the hay untouched.

"What is the matter with you, my good steed? What grieves you?"

"I grieve for us both, for I foresee a long and perilous journey."

"You are right, old fellow, but we have to go. And what is more, we have to take away and bring here old Yaga's guzla; and how shall we do it, seeing that she knows us?"

"We shall certainly succeed if you do as I tell you."

Then the horse gave him certain instructions, and when

Niezguinek had led him out of the stable and mounted he
said :

> " Marvel of strength and of beauty so white,
>   Horse of my heart, do not wait on the road ;
>   Rise in the air, like a bird take thy flight,
>   Haste to the wicked old Yaga's abode."

The horse arose in the air as if he heard some one calling
to him from the clouds, and flitting rapidly along passed over
several kingdoms within a few hours, thus reaching old Yaga's
dwelling before midnight.   Niezguinek threw the leaves of
Sleep in at the window, and by means of another wonderful
herb caused all the doors of the house to open.   On entering
he found old Yaga fast asleep, with her trough and iron
crutches beside her, while above her head hung the magic
sword and guzla.

While the old witch lay snoring with all her might, Niezguinek took the guzla and leapt on his horse, crying :

> " Marvel of strength and of beauty so white,
>   Horse of my heart, while I sing,
>   Rise in the air, like a bird take thy flight,
>   Haste to the court of my king."

Just as if the horse had seen something in the clouds, he
rose swift as an arrow, and flew through the air, above the fogs.
The same day about noon he neighed before his own manger
in the royal stable, and Niezguinek went in to the king and
presented him with the guzla.   On pronouncing the two words,
" Guzla, play," strains of music so gay and inspiriting were
heard that all the courtiers began dancing with one another.
The sick who listened were cured of their diseases, those who
were in trouble and grief forgot their sorrows, and all living

creatures were thrilled with a gladness such as they had never felt before. The king was beside himself with joy; he loaded Niezguinek with honours and presents, and, in order to have him always at court, raised him to a higher rank in the army. In this new post he had many under him, and he showed much exactitude in drill and other matters, punishing somewhat severely when necessary. He made, too, no difference in the treatment of his brothers, which angered them greatly, and caused them to be still more jealous and to plot against him. So they again imitated his handwriting and composed another letter, which they left at the king's door. When his majesty had read it he called Niezguinek to him and said, "I should much like to have the marvellous sword you speak of in your letter."

"Sire, I have not written anything about a sword," said Niezguinek.

"Well, read it for yourself." And he read:

"In a certain country within the house of old Yaga is a sword that strikes of its own accord: if the king would like to have it, I will engage to bring it him.

"(Signed)   NIEZGUINEK."

"Certainly," said Niezguinek, "this writing resembles mine, but I never wrote those words."

"Never mind, as you succeeded in bringing me the guzla you will find no difficulty in obtaining the sword. Start without delay, and do not return without it at your peril."

Niezguinek bowed and went to the stable, where he found his horse looking very thin and miserable, with his head drooping.

"What is the matter, my horse? Do you want anything?"

"I am unhappy because I foresee a long and dangerous journey."

"You are right, for we are ordered to return to Yaga's house for the sword: but how can we get hold of it? doubtless she guards it as the apple of her eye."

The horse answered, "Do as I tell you and all will be right." And he gave him certain instructions. Niezguinek came out of the stable, saddled his friend, and mounting him said:

> "Marvel of strength and of beauty so white;
> Horse of my heart, do not wait on the road;
> Rise in the air, like a bird take thy flight,
> Haste to the wicked old witch's abode."

The horse rose immediately as if he had been beckoned to by some one in the clouds, and passing swiftly through the air, crossed rivers and mountains, till at midnight he stopped before old Yaga's house.

Since the disappearance of the guzla the sword had been placed on guard before the house, and whoever came near it was cut to pieces.

Niezguinek traced a circle with holy chalk, and placing himself on horseback in the centre of it, said:

> "Sword who of thyself can smite,
> I come to brave thy ire;
> Peace or war upon this site
> Of thee I do require.
> If thou canst conquer, thine my life;
> Should I beat thee, then ends this strife."

The sword clinked, leapt into the air, and fell to the ground divided into a thousand other swords, which ranged themselves in battle array and began to attack Niezguinek. But in vain; they were powerless to touch him; for on reaching the chalk-traced circle they broke like wisps of straw. Then the sword-in-chief, seeing how useless it was to go on trying to wound him, submitted itself to Niezguinek and promised him obedience. Taking the magic weapon in his hand, he mounted his horse and said:

> "Marvel of strength and of beauty so white,
> Horse of my heart, while I sing,
> Rise in the air, like a bird take thy flight,
> Back to the court of my king."

The horse started with renewed courage, and by noon was eating his hay in the royal stables. Niezguinek went in to the king and presented him with the sword. While he was rejoicing over it one of his servants rushed in quite out of breath and said, "Sire, your enemies who attacked us last year, and whose king is your prisoner, surround our town. Being unable to redeem their sovereign, they have come with an immense army, and threaten to destroy us if their king is not released without ransom."

The king armed himself with the magic sword, and going outside the city walls, said to it, as he pointed to the enemy's camp, "Magic Sword, smite the foe."

Immediately the sword clinked, leapt flashing in the air, and fell in a thousand blades that threw themselves on the camp. One regiment was destroyed during the first attack, another was defeated in the same way, while the rest of the

terrified soldiers fled and completely disappeared.   Then the
king said, "Sword, return to me."

The thousand swords again became one, and so it returned
to its master's hand.

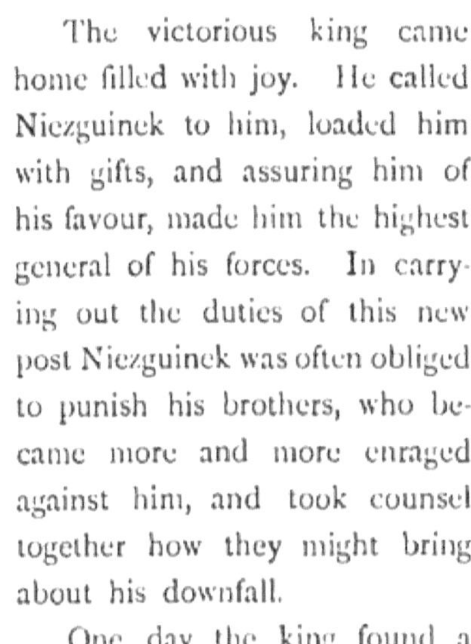

The victorious king came
home filled with joy. He called
Niezguinek to him, loaded him
with gifts, and assuring him of
his favour, made him the highest
general of his forces. In carrying out the duties of this new
post Niezguinek was often obliged
to punish his brothers, who became more and more enraged
against him, and took counsel
together how they might bring
about his downfall.

One day the king found a
letter by his door, and after read-
ing it he called Niezguinek to him
and said, "I should very much
like to see Princess Sudolisu,
whom you wish to bring me."

"Sire, I do not know the
lady, and have never spoken
to her."

"Here, look at your letter."

Niezguinek read :

"Beyond the nine kingdoms, far beyond the ocean, within

a silver vessel with golden masts lives Princess Sudolisu.　If the king wishes it, I will seek her for him.

"(Signed)　　NIEZGUINEK."

"It is true the writing is like unto mine; nevertheless, I neither composed the letter nor wrote it."

"No matter," answered the king.　"You will be able to get this princess, as you did the guzla and the sword: if not, I will have you killed."

Niezguinek bowed and went out.　He entered the stable where stood his horse looking very weak and sad, with his head bent down.

"What is the matter, dear horse?　Are you in want of anything?"

"I am sorrowful," answered the horse, "because I foresee a long and difficult journey."

"You are right, for we have to go beyond the nine kingdoms, and far beyond the ocean, to find Princess Sudolisu.　Can you tell me what to do?"

"I will do my best, and if it is God's will we shall succeed.　Bring your club of four hundred and eighty pounds weight, and let us be off."

Niezguinek saddled his horse, took his club, and mounting said:

> "Marvel of strength and of beauty so white,
>> Horse of my heart, do not lag on the road;
>> Rise in the air, through the clouds take thy flight,
>> Haste to Princess Sudolisu's abode."

Then the horse looked up as if there were something he wanted in the clouds, and with a spring flew through the air, swift as an arrow; and so by the second day they had passed over ten kingdoms, and finding themselves beyond the ocean, halted on the shore. Here the horse said to Niezguinek, "Do you see that silver ship with golden masts that rides on the waves yonder? That beautiful vessel is the home of Princess Sudolisu, youngest daughter of old Yaga. For after the witch had lost the guzla and magic sword she feared to lose her daughter too: so she shut her up in that vessel, and having thrown the key thereof into the ocean, sat herself in her oaken trough, where with the help of the iron crutches she rows round and round the silver ship, warding off tempests, and keeping at a distance all other ships that would approach it.

"'The first thing to be done is to get the diamond key that opens the ship. In order to procure this you must kill me, and then throw into the water one end of my entrails, by which bait you will trap the King of the Lobsters. Do not set him free until he has promised to get you the key, for it is this key that draws the vessel to you of its own accord."

"Ah, my beloved steed," cried Niezguinek, "how can I kill you when I love you as my own brother, and when my fate depends upon you entirely?"

"Do as I tell you; you can bring me to life again, as you did before."

Niezguinek caressed his horse, kissed him and wept over him; then, raising his mighty club, struck him full on the forehead. The poor creature staggered and fell down dead. Niezguinek cut him open, and putting an end of his entrails in the water, he kept hold of it and hid

R

himself in the water-rushes. Soon there came a crowd of crawfish, and amongst them a gigantic lobster as large as a year-old calf. Niezguinek seized him and threw him on the beach. The lobster said, "I am king of all the crawfish tribe. Let me go, and I will give you great riches for my ransom."

"I do not want your riches," answered Niezguinek, "but in exchange for your freedom give me the diamond key which belongs to the silver ship with the golden masts, for in that vessel dwells Princess Sudolisu."

The King of the Crawfish whistled, upon which myriads of his subjects appeared. He spoke to them in their own language, and dismissed one, who soon returned with the magic diamond key in his claws.

Niezguinek loosed the King of the Crawfish; and hiding himself inside his horse's body as he had been instructed, lay in wait. At that moment an old raven, followed by all his nestlings, happened to pass, and attracted by the horse's carcase, he called to his young ones to come and feast with him. Niezguinek seized the smallest of the birds and held it firmly.

"Let my birdling go," said the old raven, "I will give you in return anything you like to ask."

"Fetch me then three kinds of water, the Life-giving, the Curing, and the Strengthening."

The old raven started off, and while awaiting his return Niezguinek, who still held the ravenling, questioned him as to where he had come from and what he had seen on his travels, and in this way heard news of his brothers.

When the father bird returned, carrying with him the

bottles filled with the marvellous waters, he wanted to have his nestling back.

"One moment more," said Niezguinek, "I want to be sure that they are of the right sort."

Then he replaced the entrails in the body of his horse and sprinkled him first with the Life-giving, then with the Curing, and finally with the Strengthening Water; after which his beloved steed leapt to his feet full of strength and cried, "Ah! how very soundly I have slept."

Niezguinek released the young raven and said to his horse, "For sure, you would have slept to all eternity, and have never seen the sun again, if I had not revived you as you taught me."

While speaking he saw the marvellous ship sparkling white in the sun. She was made entirely of pure silver, with golden masts. The rigging was of silk, the sails of velvet, and the whole was enclosed in a casing of inpenetrable steel network. Niezguinek sprang down to the water's edge armed with his club, and rubbing his forehead with the diamond key, said:

> " Riding on the ocean waves a magic ship I see ;
>   Stop and change thy course, O ship, here I hold the key.
>   Obey the signal known to thee,
>   And come at once direct to me."

The vessel turned right round and came at full speed towards land, and right on to the bank, where it remained motionless.

Niezguinek smashed in the steel network with his club; and opening the doors with the diamond key, there found

Princess Sudolisu.　He made her unconscious with the herb
Sleep, and lifting her before him on his horse, said :

> "Marvel of strength and of beauty so white,
> Horse of my heart, while I sing,
> Swift as an arrow through space take thy flight
> Straight to the court of my king."

Then the horse, as if he saw some strange thing in the
clouds, lifted himself in the air and began to fly through
space so rapidly that in about two hours he had crossed
rivers, mountains, and forests, and had reached his journey's
end.

Although Niezguinek had fallen violently in love with the
princess himself, he took her straight to the royal palace and
introduced her to the king.

Now she was so exquisitely beautiful that the monarch
was quite dazzled by looking at her. and being thus carried
away by his admiration, he put his arm round her as if to
caress her : but she rebuked him severely.

"What have I done to offend you, princess? Why do
you treat me so harshly?"

"Because in spite of your rank you are ill-bred. You
neither ask my name nor that of my parents, and you
think to take possession of me as if I were but a dog or a
falcon. You must understand that he who would be my
husband must have triple youth, that of heart, soul, and
body."

"Charming princess, if I could become young again we
would be married directly."

She replied, "But I have the means of making you so,

and by help of this sword in my hand. For with it I will pierce you to the heart, then cut up your body into small pieces, wash them carefully, and join them together again. And if I breathe upon them you will return to life young and handsome, just as if you were only twenty years of age."

"Oh indeed! I should like to know who would submit to that; first make trial of Sir Niezguinek here."

The princess looked at him, whereupon he bowed and said, "Lovely princess, I willingly submit, although I am young enough without it. In any case life without you would be valueless."

Then the princess took a step towards him and killed him with her sword. She cut him up in pieces and washed these in pure water, after which she joined them together again and breathed upon them. Instantly Niezguinek sprang up full of life and health, and looked so handsome and bright that the old king, who was dreadfully jealous, exclaimed, "Make me, too, young again, princess; do not lose a moment."

The princess pierced him to the heart with her sword, cut him up into little pieces, and, opening the window, threw them out, at the same time calling the king's dogs, who quickly ate them up. Then she turned to Niezguinek and said, "Proclaim yourself king, and I will be your queen."

He followed her advice, and within a short time they were married; his brothers, whom he had pardoned, and his parents having been invited to the wedding. On their way back from the church the magic sword suddenly clinked, and, flashing in the air, divided itself into a thousand swords that placed themselves on guard as sentinels all round the palace. The guzla, too, began to play so sweetly and gaily that every living thing began to dance for joy.

The festival was magnificent. I myself was there, and drank freely of wine and mead; and although not a drop went into my mouth, my chin was quite wet.

OHNIVAK

OHNIVAK

OHNIVÁK

A CERTAIN king had a beautiful garden which contained a number of very rare trees, but the most rare
of all was an apple tree. It stood in the middle of the
garden, and produced one golden apple every day. In the
morning the blossom unfolded, during the day you might
watch the fruit grow, and before nightfall the apple was fully
ripe. The next day the same thing occurred—indeed, it
happened regularly every twenty-four hours. Nevertheless,

no ripe fruit ever remained on the tree on the following day; the apple disappeared, no one knew how or when, and this deeply grieved the king.

At last he could bear it no longer, and calling his eldest son to him, said: "My child, I wish you to keep watch in the garden to-night, and see if you can find out what becomes of my golden apples. I will reward you with the choice of all my treasures; if you should be lucky enough to get hold of the thief, and bring him to me, I would gladly give you half my kingdom."

The young prince girded his trusty sword to his side, and with his crossbow on his shoulder and a good stock of well-tempered arrows, went into the garden to mount guard. And as he sat under the apple tree a great drowsiness came over him which he could not resist; his arms dropped, his eyes closed, and stretching himself on the grass he slept as soundly as if he had been in his own bed at home, nor did he awake until day dawn, and then he saw that the apple had disappeared.

When questioned by his father, he said that no thieves had come, but that the apple had vanished all the same. The king shook his head, for he did not believe a word of it. Then, turning to his second son, he bade him keep watch, and promised him a handsome reward if he should catch the thief.

So the second son armed himself with everything necessary and went into the garden. But he succeeded no better than his brother, for he could not resist the desire to sleep, and when he awoke the apple was no longer there.

When his father asked him how it disappeared, he replied, "No one took it, it vanished of itself."

"Now, my dearest one, take your turn," said the king to his youngest son; "although you are young, and have less experience than your brothers, let us see if you cannot succeed where they have failed. If you are willing, go, and may God help you."

Towards evening, when it began to be dusk, the youngest son went into the garden to keep watch. He took with him a sword and crossbow, a few well-tempered arrows, and a hedgehog's skin as a sort of apron, for he thought that while sitting under the tree, if he spread the skin over his knees, the pricking of the bristles on his hands might keep him awake. And so it did, for by this means he was able to resist the drowsiness that came over him.

At midnight Ohnivak, the bird of fire, flew down and alighted upon the tree, and was just going off with the apple when the prince fixed an arrow to his bow, and letting it fly, struck the bird under the wing. Although wounded, it flew away, dropping one of its feathers upon the ground. That night for the first time the apple remained untouched upon the tree.

"Have you caught the thief?" asked the king next day.

"Not altogether, but no doubt we shall have him in time. I have a bit of his trappings." And he gave the king the feather, and told him all that had taken place.

The king was charmed with the feather; so lovely and bright was it that it illumined all the galleries of the palace, and they needed no other light.

The courtiers told the king that the feather could only belong to Ohnivak, the bird of fire, and that it was worth all the rest of the royal treasures put together.

From that time Ohnivak came no more to the garden, and the apples remained untouched. Yet the king could think of nothing else but how to possess this marvellous bird. At last, beginning to despair of ever seeing it, he was filled with melancholy, and would remain for hours in deep thought; thus he became really ill, and every day continued to grow worse.

One day he summoned his three sons before him and said, "My dear children. you see the sad state I am in. If I could but hear the bird Ohnivak sing just once I should be cured of this disease of the heart; otherwise it will be my death. Whichever of you shall succeed in catching Ohnivak alive and inducing him to sing to me, to him I will give half of my kingdom and the heirship to the throne."

Having taken leave of their father the brothers set off. They travelled together until they came to a part of the forest where the road branched off in three directions.

"Which turning shall we take?" asked the eldest.

The second brother answered, "We are three, and three roads lie before us; let us each choose one, thus we shall treble our chances of finding the bird, for we shall seek it in three different countries."

"That is a good idea, but how shall each one decide which way to choose?"

The youngest brother said, "I will leave the choice to you two, and will take whichever road you leave me."

So each took the road that chance decided for him, agreeing that when their mission was over they would return to the point of departure. In order to recognise the place again each one planted the branch of a tree at the cross

roads, and they believed that he whose branch should take root and grow into a big tree would be successful in the quest.

When each one had planted his branch at the chosen road they started off. The eldest rode on, and never stopped until he reached the top of a high mountain; there he dismounted, and let his horse graze while he ate his breakfast. Suddenly a red fox came up, and speaking in the language of men, said: "Pray, my handsome prince, give me a little of what you are eating; I am very hungry."

For answer the prince let fly an arrow from his crossbow, but it is impossible to say whether he hit the fox for it vanished and did not appear again.

The second brother, without meeting with any adventure, reached a wide-stretching moor, where he stopped for his meal. The red fox appeared to him and begged for food; but he also refused food to the famished fox, and shot at him. The creature disappeared as before.

The youngest travelled on till he came to the banks of a river. Feeling tired and hungry, he got down from his horse and began his breakfast; while he was eating, up came the red fox.

"Please, young sir," said the fox, "give me a morsel to satisfy my hunger."

The prince threw him a piece of meat, and spoke kindly to him.

"Come near, do not be afraid, my red fox; I see you are more hungry than I, but there is enough for us both."

And he divided all his provisions into two equal parts, one for himself, and one for the poor red fox.

When the latter had eaten to his heart's content, he said:

"You have fed me well, in return I will serve you well; mount your horse and follow me. If you do everything I tell you, the Bird of Fire shall be yours."

Then he set off at a run before the horseman, clearing the road for him with his bushy tail. By means of this marvellous broom, mountains were cut down, ravines filled up, and rivers bridged over.

The young prince followed at a gallop, without the slightest wish to stop, until they came to a castle built of copper.

"The Bird of Fire is in this castle," said the fox; "you must enter exactly at midday, for then the guards will be asleep, and you will pass unnoticed. Above all, beware of stopping anywhere. In the first apartment you will find twelve birds black as night, in golden cages; in the second, twelve golden birds in wooden cages; in the third, Ohnivak, the bird of fire, roosting on his perch. Near him are two cages, one of wood and the other of gold; be sure you put him in the wooden cage—you would be sorry for it if he were put into the golden one."

The prince entered the castle, and found everything just as the fox had told him. Having passed through the two rooms he came to the third, and there saw the fire-bird on his perch, apparently asleep. It was indeed a beautiful creature, so beautiful that the prince's heart beat high with joy. He handled him without difficulty, and put him into the wooden cage, thinking at the same time to himself that it could hardly be right for so lovely a bird to be in such an ugly cage, a golden cage could be the only right place for him. So he took him out of the wooden cage and placed him in the golden one. Hardly had he shut the door when the bird opened his eyes and gave a piercing scream; so shrill was it that it awoke the other birds, who began to sing as loud as they could, and gave the alarm to the guards at the palace door. These rushed in, seized the prince, and dragged him before the king. The latter was very angry, and said: "Infamous thief, who are you to have dared to force an entrance, and pass through my sentinels, to steal my bird Ohnivak?"

"I am not a thief," answered the young prince indignantly, "I have come to reclaim a thief whom you protect. I am the son of a king, and in my father's gardens is an apple tree that bears golden fruit. It blossoms at morning-time, while during the day the flower develops into an apple that grows and ripens after sunset. Now in the night your bird robbed us of our golden apples, and though I watched and wounded him I could not catch him. My father is dying with grief because of this, and the only remedy that can save and restore him to health, is that he may listen to the fire-bird's song. This is why I beg your majesty to give him me."

"You may have him," said the king, "but on one condition, that you bring me Zlato-Nrivak, the horse with the golden mane."

So the prince had to go away empty-handed.

"Why did you not do as I told you? Why must you go and take the golden cage?" said the fox, in despair at the failure of the expedition.

"I admit it was my own fault," said the prince, "but do not punish me by being angry. I want your advice: tell me how I am to get Zlato-Nrivak?"

"I know how it can be done," answered the red fox,

"and I will help you once more. Get on your horse, follow me, and do as I tell you."

The fox ran on in front, clearing the road with his bushy tail. The prince followed at a gallop, until they came to a castle built entirely of silver.

"In that castle lives the Horse with the Golden Mane," said the fox. "You will have to go exactly at midday, when the sentinels are asleep; thus you will get past safe and sound. But mind, do not stop anywhere. You must pass through three stables. In the first are twelve black horses with golden bridles; in the second, twelve white horses with black bridles; in the third stands Zlato-Nrivak in front of his manger, while near him are two bridles, one of gold, the other of black leather. Whatever you do, beware of using the first, for you will surely repent it."

The prince waited until the appointed time and then entered the castle, finding everything exactly as the fox had said. In the third stable stood Zlato-Nrivak, eating fire that flared up out of his silver trough.

The Horse with the Golden Mane was so beautiful that the prince could not take his eyes off him. Quickly unhooking the black leather bridle, he put it over the horse's head. The animal made no resistance, but was gentle and quiet as a lamb. Then the prince looked covetously at the golden bridle sparkling with gems, and said to himself, "It is a shame that such a splendid creature should be guided by these ugly black reins while there is a bridle here far more suited to him, and that is indeed his by right." So, forgetting his late experience and the warnings of the red fox, he tore off the black bridle and put in its place that of gold set with precious stones. No sooner did the horse feel the change than he began to neigh and caper about, while all the other horses answered with a perfect storm of neighings. The sentinels, aroused by the noise, ran in, and seizing the prince, led him before the king.

"Insolent thief," cried the enraged monarch, "how is it that you have escaped the vigilance of the guards and have dared to lay hands upon my horse with the golden mane? It is really disgraceful."

"True, I am nothing better," replied the prince proudly, "but I was forced to do it against my will." And he related all his misadventures at the copper castle, adding that it was impossible to obtain the fire-bird except in exchange for Zlato-Nrivak, and that he hoped his majesty would make him a present of the horse.

"Most willingly," answered the king, "but on one condition, that you bring me the Maiden with the Golden Locks: she lives in the golden castle on the shores of the Black Sea."

The fox was waiting in the forest the prince's return, and when he saw him come back without the horse he was very angry indeed.

"Did I not warn you," said he, "to be content with the black leather bridle? It is really a loss of time to try and help such an ungrateful fellow, for it seems impossible to make you hear reason."

"Don't be cross," said the prince, "I confess that I am in fault; I ought to have obeyed your orders. But have a little more patience with me and help me out of this difficulty."

"Very well; but this will certainly be the last time. If

you do just as you are told we may yet repair all that has been spoilt by your imprudence. Mount your horse and follow—off!"

The fox ran on in front, clearing the road with his bushy tail, until they reached the shores of the Black Sea.

"That palace yonder," said the fox, "is the residence of the Queen of the Ocean Kingdom. She has three daughters; it is the youngest who has the golden hair, and is called Zlato-Vlaska. Now you must first go to the queen and ask her to give you one of her daughters in marriage. If she takes kindly to your proposal she will bid you choose, and mind you take that princess who is the most plainly dressed."

The queen received him most graciously, and when he explained the object of his visit she led him into a room where the three daughters were spinning.

They were so much alike that no one could possibly distinguish one from the other, and they were all so marvellously lovely that when the young prince looked upon them he dared hardly breathe. Their hair was carefully covered by a veil through which one could not distinguish the colour of it, but their dresses were different. The first wore a gown and veil embroidered with gold, and used a golden distaff; the second had on a gown embroidered with silver and held a distaff of the same metal; the third wore a gown and veil of dazzling whiteness, and her distaff was made of wood.

The mother bade the prince choose, whereupon he pointed to the maiden clothed in white, saying, "Give me this one to wife."

"Ah," said the queen, "some one has been letting you

into the secret: but wait a little, we shall meet again to-morrow."

All that night the prince lay awake, wondering how he should manage not to make a mistake on the morrow. At dawn he was already at the palace gates, which he had hardly entered when the princess clothed in white chanced to pass: it was Zlato-Vlaska, and she had come to meet him.

"If it is your wish to choose me again to-day," she said, "observe carefully, and take the maiden around whose head buzzes a small fly."

In the afternoon the queen took the prince into a room where her three daughters sat, and said: "If among these princesses you recognise the one you chose yesterday she shall be yours; if not, you must die."

The young girls stood side by side, dressed alike in costly robes, and all had golden hair. The prince was puzzled, and their beauty and splendour dazzled him. For some time he could hardly see distinctly; then, all of a sudden, a small fly buzzed over the head of one of the princesses.

"This is the maiden who belongs to me," cried he, "and whom I chose yesterday."

The queen, astonished that he should have guessed correctly, said, "Quite right, but I cannot let you have her until you have submitted to another trial, which shall be explained to you to-morrow."

On the morrow she pointed out to him a large fish-pond which lay in the forest, and giving him a small golden sieve, said: "If with this sieve you can, before sunset, empty that fish-pond yonder, I will give you my daughter with the golden hair, but if you fail you will lose your life."

The prince took the sieve, and, going down to the pond,
plunged it in to try his luck; but no sooner had he lifted it
up than all the water ran out through the holes—not a drop
was left behind. Not knowing what to do, he sat down on
the bank with the sieve in his hand, wondering in what
possible way the difficulty might be overcome.

"Why are you so sad?" asked the maiden in white, as
she came towards him.

"Because I fear you will never be mine," sighed he;
"your mother has given me an impossible task."

"Come, cheer up, away with fear; it will all be right in
the end."

Thereupon she took the sieve and threw it into the fish-
pond. Instantly the water turned to foam on the surface,
and a thick vapour rose up, which fell in a fog so dense that
nothing could be seen through it. Then the prince heard
footsteps, and turning round saw his horse coming towards
him, with his bridle down and the red fox at his side.

"Mount quickly," said the horse, "there is not a moment
to lose; lift the maiden in front of you."

The faithful steed flew like an arrow, and sped rapidly
along over the road that had been recently cleared by the
bushy tail of the red fox. But this time, instead of leading,
the red fox followed, his tail working marvels as he went: it
destroyed the bridges, reopened the ravines, raised high mountains, and in fact put back everything as it used to be.

The prince felt very happy as he rode along, holding the
Princess with the Golden Hair, but it saddened him much to
think he would have to give up all thought of marrying her
himself, and that within a few short hours he must leave her

with the king of the silver palace: the nearer he came to it, the more wretched he grew. The red fox, who noticed this, said: "It appears to me that you do not want to exchange the lovely Zlato-Vlaska for the Horse with the Golden Mane: is it not so? Well, I have helped you so far, I will see what I can do for you now."

And having thus spoken he turned a somersault over the stump of a fallen tree which lay in the forest: while, to the prince's amazement, he was immediately transformed into a young girl exactly resembling the Princess with the Golden Hair.

"Now, leave your real bride in the forest," said the transformed fox, "and take me with you to offer to the king of the silver palace in exchange for his horse Zlato-Nrivak. Mount the horse, return here, and escape with the maid you love; I will manage the rest."

The king of the silver castle received the maiden without the least suspicion, and handed over in exchange the Horse with the Golden Mane, over whose back lay the bejewelled bridle. The prince left at once.

At the palace all were busy preparing the wedding feast, for the marriage was to take place immediately, and everything was to be of the most costly description. Invitations had been out to all the grandees of the land.

Towards the end of the feast, when every one had drunk his fill of wine and pleasure, the king asked his guests their opinions on the charms of his bride.

"She is most beautiful," said one, "in fact, it would be impossible for her to be more lovely; only, it seems to me that her eyes are somewhat like those of a fox."

The words were hardly out of his mouth when the royal bride vanished, while in her place sat a red fox, who with one vigorous bound sprang through the door and disappeared to rejoin the prince, who had hastened on in front. With sweeping strokes of his bushy tail he overthrew bridges, reopened precipices, and heaped up mountains; but it was very hard work for the poor thing, and he did not come up with the runaways until they had almost reached the copper castle. Here they all had a rest, while the red fox turned a somersault and transformed himself into a horse resembling the one with the golden mane. Then the prince entered the copper castle and exchanged the transformed fox for the fire-bird Ohnivak, the king having no suspicions whatever. The red fox, having thus deceived the monarch, reassumed his own shape and hurried after the departing prince, whom he did not overtake until they had reached the banks of the river where they had first become acquainted.

"Now here you are, prince," said the red fox, "in possession of Ohnivak, of the lovely Zlato-Vlaska, and of the Horse with the Golden Mane. Henceforth you can manage without my help, so return to your father's house in peace and joy; but, take warning, do not stop anywhere on the way, for if you do some misfortune will overtake you."

With these words the red fox vanished, while the prince continued his journey unhindered. In his hand he held the golden cage that contained the fire-bird, and at his side the lovely Zlato-Vlaska rode the Horse with the Golden Mane; truly, he was the happiest of men.

When he reached the cross roads where he had parted from his brothers, he hastened to look for the branches they

had planted. His alone had become a spreading tree, theirs
were both withered. Delighted with this proof of divine
favour, he felt a strong desire to rest for a while under the
shadow of his own tree; he therefore dismounted, and assist-
ing the princess to do the same, fastened their horses to
one of the branches and hung up the cage containing
Ohnivak on another: within a few moments they were all
sound asleep.

Meanwhile the two elder brothers arrived at the same
place by different roads, and both with empty hands. There
they found their two branches withered, that of their brother
having grown into a splendid tree. Under the shade of the
latter he lay sleeping; by his side was the Maid with the
Golden Locks; the horse, Zlato-Nrivak, was fastened to a tree,
and the fire-bird roosted in his golden cage.

The hearts of the two brothers were filled with envious
and wicked thoughts, and they whispered thus to one another,
"Just think what will become of us—the youngest will receive
half of the kingdom during our father's life and succeed to the
throne at his death; why not cut his throat at once? One of
us will take the Maid with the Golden Locks, the other can
carry the bird to our father and keep the Horse with the Golden
Mane; as for the kingdom, we will divide it between us."

After this debate they killed their youngest brother and
cut up his body into small pieces, while they threatened to
treat Zlato-Vlaska in the same way if she attempted to disobey them.

On reaching home they sent the Horse with the Golden
Mane to the marble stables, the cage containing Ohnivak was
placed in the room where their father lay sick, and the princess

was allowed a beautiful suite of apartments and maids of honour to attend her.

When the king, who was much weakened by suffering, had looked at the bird, he asked after his youngest son. To which the brothers replied: "We have not seen or heard anything of him, it is very likely that he has been killed."

The poor old man was much affected—it seemed, indeed, as if his last hour had come. The fire-bird moped and refused to sing; the Horse with the Golden Mane stood with his head bent down before his manger, and would eat no food; while Princess Zlato-Vlaska remained as silent as if she had been born dumb, her beautiful hair was neglected and uncombed, and she wept—her tears fell fast.

Now as the red fox chanced to pass through the forest he came upon the mangled body of the youngest brother, and he at once set to work to put the scattered pieces together, but was unable to restore them to life. At that moment a raven, accompanied by two young ones, came hovering overhead. The fox crouched behind a bramble bush; and when one of the young birds alighted upon the body to feed, he seized it and made a pretence of strangling it. Upon which the parent bird, full of anxious love and fear, perched upon a branch close by and croaked as if to say, "Let my poor little nestling go. I have done you no harm, neither have I worried you; let him free, and I will take the first opportunity of returning your kindness."

"Just so," replied the red fox, "for I am greatly in need of some kindness. Now if you will fetch me some of the Water of Death, and some of the Water of Life, from the Red Sea, I will let your nestling go safe and sound."

The old raven promised to fetch the water, and went off at once.

Within three days he returned, carrying in his beak two small bottles, one full of the Water of Death, the other of the Water of Life. When the red fox received them he wished first to try their effect upon some living creature, so he cut the small raven up, and joining the pieces together, watered them with the Water of Death. Instantly they became a living bird, without mark or join anywhere. This he sprinkled with the Water of Life, upon which the young raven spread its wings and flew off to its family.

The red fox then performed the same operation on the body of the young prince, and with the same happy result, for he rose again perfect in form, and having about him no wound scars. On coming to life again, all he said was, "Dear me! What a pleasant sleep I have had."

"I believe you," replied the red fox, "you would have gone on sleeping for ever if I had not awakened you. And what a foolish young man you are: did I not particularly order you not to stop anywhere, but to go straight back to your father's house?"

He then related all that his brothers had done, and having obtained a peasant's dress for him, led him to the outskirts of the forest, close to the royal palace, where he left him.

The young prince then entered the palace grounds, un-recognised by the servants, and on representing that he was in need of employment, was appointed stable-boy to the royal stables. Some little time after he heard the grooms lamenting that the Horse with the Golden Mane would eat no food.

"What a pity it is," said they, "that this splendid steed should starve to death; he droops his head and will take nothing."

"Give him," said the disguised prince, "some pea-straw; I bet you anything he will eat that."

"But do you really think so? Why, our rough draught horses would refuse such coarse food."

The prince's only answer was to fetch a bundle of pea-straw, which he put into Zlato-Nrivak's marble trough : then, passing his hand gently over his neck and mane, he said to him, "Grieve no more, my horse with the golden mane."

The beautiful creature recognised his master's voice, and neighing with joy, greedily devoured the pea-straw.

The news was noised about from one end of the palace to the other, and the sick king summoned the boy to his presence.

"I hear you have made Zlato-Nrivak eat," said his majesty; "do you think you could make my fire-bird sing? Go and examine him closely: he is very sad, he droops his wings, and will neither eat nor drink. Ah me! if he dies I shall certainly die too."

"Your majesty may rest assured, the bird will not die. Let him have some husks of barley to eat, then he will soon be all right and begin to sing."

The king ordered them to be brought, and the disguised prince put a handful into Ohnivak's cage, saying, "Cheer up, my fire-bird."

As soon as Ohnivak heard his master's voice he shook himself, and made his feathers shine with more than their usual brightness. Then he began to dance about his cage,

T

and pecking up the husks, sang so exquisitely that the
king immediately felt better, and it was as if a great weight
had been lifted off his heart. The fire-bird again burst into
song, and this so affected the king that he sat up quite well,
and embraced the disguised prince out of very gratitude.

"Now," said he, "teach me how to restore to health
this beautiful maiden with the golden hair whom my sons
brought back with them; for she will not speak a word, her
beautiful hair remains uncared for, and her tears fall night
and day."

"If your majesty will allow me to speak a few words
to her, it may be the means of making her bright and
happy."

The king himself led the way to her apartments, and
the disguised prince, taking her hand, said: "Look up a
moment, sweetheart; why these tears? And why grieve
thus, dear bride?"

The maiden knew him at once, and with a cry of joy
threw herself into his arms. This astonished the king
mightily, and he could not for the life of him think how
a stable-boy dare address such a princess as his "dear
bride."

The prince then addressed the king thus: "And are
you indeed the only one who does not know me? How
is it, my father and sovereign, that you have not recognised
your youngest son? I alone have succeeded in obtaining
the Fire-Bird, the Horse with the Golden Mane, and the
Maid with the Golden Hair."

Thereupon he related all his adventures, and Zlato-Vlaska
in her turn told how the wicked brothers had threatened

to kill her if she betrayed them. As for these bad men, they shook from head to foot, and trembled like leaves in the wind. The indignant king ordered them to be executed then and there.

Not very long after these events the youngest prince married the beautiful Zlato-Vlaska, and the king gave him half of his kingdom as a wedding present. When the old king died he reigned in his stead, and lived happily with the princess ever after.

TEARS OF PEARLS

TEARS OF PEARLS

TEARS OF PEARLS

ONCE upon a time there lived a very rich widow, with whom lived three children—a handsome stepson; his sister, who was marvellously beautiful; and her own daughter, passably good-looking.

All three children lived under the same roof, but, as is often the case where there are step-parents, they were treated very differently. The lady's own daughter was bad-tempered, disobedient, vain, and of a tell-tale disposition: yet she was made much of, praised, and caressed. The step-children were treated very harshly: the boy, kind-hearted and obliging, was made to do all sorts of hard unpleasant work, was constantly scolded, and looked upon as a good-for-nothing. The step-daughter, who was not only exceedingly pretty but was as sweet as an angel, was found fault with on all occasions, and her life made utterly miserable.

It is, after all, but natural to love one's own children better than those of others, but the feeling of love should be governed by the laws of fairness. Now this wicked woman was blind to the faults of the child she loved, and to the good qualities of her husband's children, whom she hated.

When in a bad temper she was fond of boasting of the handsome fortune she intended securing for her own daughter, even though the step-children should be unprovided for. But, as the old proverb says, "Man proposes, but God disposes." We shall therefore see how things turned out.

One Sunday morning, before going to church, the step-daughter went into the garden to pick some flowers for decorating the altar. She had only gathered a few roses when, looking up, she saw quite close to her three young men robed in dazzling white garments. They sat on a bench shaded by shrubs, while near them was an old man who asked her for alms.

She felt rather nervous before the strangers, but when she saw the old man she took her last penny from her purse and gave it him. He thanked her, and raising his hand over the girl's head, said to the men: "This orphan girl is pious, patient under misfortune, and kind to the poor, with whom she shares the little she has. Tell me what you wish for her."

The first said, "I wish that when she weeps her tears may be changed into so many pearls."

"And I," replied the second, "that when she smiles sweet roses may fall from her lips."

"My wish," said the third, "is that whenever she dips her hands into water there shall appear in it shining gold-fish."

"All these gifts shall be hers," added the old man. And with these words they vanished.

The maiden was filled with awe, and fell on her knees in prayer. Then her heart was filled with joy and peace, and she went back into the house. She had scarcely crossed the threshold when her stepmother came forward, and looking at her sternly, said, "Well, where have you been?"

The poor child began to cry, when—marvel of marvels— instead of tears, pearls fell from her eyes.

Notwithstanding her rage, the stepmother picked them up as quickly as possible, while the girl smiled as she watched her. And as she smiled roses fell from her lips, and her stepmother was beside herself with delight.

The girl then went to put the flowers she had gathered in water; and as she dipped her fingers in it while arranging them, pretty little gold-fish appeared in the bowl.

From that day these marvels were constantly occurring; the tears were changed into pearls, the smiles scattered roses, and the water, even if she dipped but the tips of her fingers in, was filled with gold-fish.

The stepmother softened and became more gentle, while little by little she managed to draw from her step-child the secret of these gifts.

So next Sunday morning she sent her own daughter into

the garden to gather flowers, under pretence of their being for the altar. When she had picked a few, she raised her eyes and saw the three young men sitting on a low seat, while near them stood the little old man with white hair, begging for alms. She pretended to be shy before the young men, but at the beggar's request drew from her pocket a gold piece, and gave it him, evidently much against her will. He put it in his pocket, and turning to his companions, said: "This girl is the spoilt child of her mother; she is bad-tempered and naughty, while her heart is hardened against the poor. It is easy to understand why, for the first time in her life, she has been so generous to-day. Tell me what gifts you would wish me to bestow upon her."

The first said, "May her tears be changed into lizards."

"And her smile produce hideous toads," added the second.

"And when her hands touch the water may it be filled with serpents," said the third.

"So let it be," cried the old man. And they all vanished.

The poor girl was terrified, and went back to tell her mother what had happened. And it was even so; for if she smiled hideous toads fell from her mouth, her tears were changed into lizards, and the water in which she dipped but the tips of her fingers was filled with serpents.

The stepmother was in despair, but she only loved her child the more, and hated the orphans with a yet more bitter hatred. Indeed, she worried them to such an extent that the boy determined to put up with it no longer, but to seek his fortune elsewhere. So he tied up his belongings in a hand-kerchief, took a loving farewell of his sister, commending her to God's care, and left his home. The great world lay before him, but which path to take he knew not. Turning to the cemetery where his parents lay side by side, he wept and prayed, kissed the earth that covered them three times, and set off on his travels.

At that moment he felt something hard in the folds of his tunic, and pressing on his heart. Wondering what it could be, he put in his hand and drew thence a charming portrait of his dearly loved sister, surrounded with pearls, roses, and gold-fish. So great was his astonishment he could hardly believe his eyes. But he was very happy, and kissed the picture over and over again ; then, with one more look at the cemetery, he made the sign of the cross and departed.

Now a beautiful story is soon told, but the acts of which it is the sum pass more slowly.

After many adventures of little importance he reached the capital of a kingdom by the sea, and there obtained the post of under-gardener at the royal palace, with good food and wages.

In his prosperity he did not forget his unhappy sister, for he felt very uneasy about her. When he had a few moments to himself he would sit down in some retired spot and gaze upon her portrait with a sad heart and eyes filled with tears. For the picture was a faithful likeness of her, and he looked upon it as a gift from his parents.

Now the king had noticed this habit of his, and one day while he sat by a stream looking at the picture he came quietly behind him, and glanced over his shoulder to see what he was so attentively regarding.

"Give me that portrait," said the monarch.

The boy handed it him. The king examined it closely,

and admiring it greatly, said : "I have never seen such a beautiful face in all my life, never even dreamed of such loveliness. Come, tell me, is the original of the picture living?"

The lad burst into tears, and told him it was the living image of his sister, who a short time since had received as a special mark of favour from God, that her tears should be changed into pearls, her smiles into roses, and the touch of her hands in water should produce beautiful gold-fish.

The king commanded him to write to his stepmother at once and bid her send her lovely step-daughter to the chapel of the palace, where the king would be waiting to marry her. The letter also contained promises of special royal favours.

The lad wrote the letter, which the king sent by a special messenger.

Now a good story is soon told, but the deeds of which it is the sum are not performed so quickly.

When the stepmother received the letter she determined to say nothing about it to her step-child, but she showed it to her own daughter, and talked the matter over with her. Then she went to learn the art of sorcery from a witch, and having found out all it was necessary to know, set off with both of the girls. On approaching the capital, the wicked woman pushed her step-child out of the carriage and repeated some magic words over her. After this she became very small and covered with feathers, then in a moment she was changed into a wild-duck. She began to quack, and made for the water, as ducks do, and swam to a far distance. The stepmother bade her farewell in the following words : "By the strength of my hate may my will be fulfilled. Swim about the banks in the form of a duck, and rejoice in thy

liberty. During that time my daughter shall take thy form, shall marry the king, and shall enjoy the good fortune fate destined for thee."

At the conclusion of these words her own child became endowed with all the graces and beauty of her unfortunate step-sister. The two then continued their journey, arriving at the royal chapel at the appointed hour. The king received them with all honours, while the deceitful woman gave away her own daughter, whom the bridegroom believed to be the original of the beautiful picture. After the ceremony the mother went away loaded with presents. The king, as he looked at his young wife, could not understand why he did not feel for her the sympathy and admiration he had felt for the portrait she so much resembled. But it could not be altered now; what is done is done. So he admired her beauty and looked forward to the pleasure of seeing pearls fall from her eyes, roses from her lips, and gold-fish at the touch of her fingers.

During the wedding feast the newly-made bride forgot herself and smiled at her husband; immediately a number of hideous toads escaped from her lips. The king, overcome with horror and disgust, rushed away from her, upon which she began to cry, but instead of pearls, lizards fell from her eyes. The majordomo ordered water to be brought for her to wash her hands, but no sooner had she dipped the tips of her fingers in the bowl than it was filled with serpents that hissed and twisted and threw themselves among the wedding guests. The panic was general, and a scene of great confusion followed. The guard was called in, and had the greatest trouble to clear the hall of the disgusting reptiles.

The bridegroom had taken refuge in the garden, and when he saw the young man coming towards him, whom he thought had deceived him, his anger overcame him, and he struck the poor lad with so much force that he fell down dead.

The queen ran forward sobbing, and taking the king by the hand, said: "What have you done? You have killed my innocent brother. It is neither my fault, nor was it his, that since the wedding I have by some enchantment lost the marvellous power I possessed before. This evil will pass away in time, but time can never restore to me my dear brother, my own mother's son."

"Forgive me, dear wife; in a moment of irritation I thought he had deceived me, and I wanted to punish him, but did not mean to kill. I regret it deeply, but it cannot be helped now. Forgive me my fault as I forgive yours, with all my heart."

"You have my forgiveness, but I beg you to see that your wife's brother has an honourable burial."

Her wishes were carried out, and the orphan lad, who had passed as her brother, was laid in a handsome coffin. The chapel was hung with black, and at night a guard was placed both inside and out.

Towards midnight the church doors silently opened, and while the guards were overcome by sleep a pretty little duck entered unnoticed. She stopped in the middle of the aisle, shook herself, and pulled out her feathers one by one. Then it took the form of the beautiful step-daughter, for it was she. She went up to her brother's coffin and stood gazing at him, and as she looked she wept sorrowfully. Then she put on her feathers again and went out a duck. When the guards awoke they were astonished to find a quantity of fine pearls in the coffin. Next day they told the king that the doors had opened of themselves towards midnight, that they had been overcome by sleep, and that on awakening they had found a large number of pearls in the coffin, but knew not how they got there. The king was very much surprised, especially at the appearance of the pearls, that ought to have been produced by his wife's tears. On the second night he doubled the guard, and impressed upon them the necessity for watch-fulness.

At midnight the doors again opened silently as before, the soldiers went to sleep, and the same little duck entered, and, taking out her feathers, appeared as a lovely maiden. She could not help smiling as she looked upon the sleeping soldiers, the number of which had been doubled on her account ; and as she smiled a number of roses fell from her lips. As she drew near her brother her tears fell in torrents, leaving a profusion of fine pearls. After some time she put on her feathers and went out a duck. When the guards awoke they took the roses and the pearls to the king. He was still more surprised to see roses with the pearls, for these roses should have fallen from his wife's lips. He again increased the number of the guard, and threatened them with the most severe punishment if they failed to watch all night. They did their best to obey, but in vain ; they could only sleep. When they awoke they found, not only roses and pearls, but little gold-fish swimming in the holy water.

The amazed king could only conclude that their sleep was caused by magic. On the fourth night he not only in-creased the number of soldiers, but, unknown to every one, hid himself behind the altar, where he hung a mirror, through which he could see everything that passed without being seen.

At midnight the doors opened. The soldiers, under the influence of sleep, had let fall their arms and lay on the ground. The king kept his eyes fixed on the mirror, through which he saw a little wild-duck enter. It looked timidly round on all sides, then, reassured at the sight of the sleeping guards, advanced to the centre of the nave and took off its feathers, thus appearing as a young maiden of exquisite beauty.

The king, overwhelmed with joy and admiration, had a presentiment that this was his true bride. So when she drew near the coffin he crept noiselessly out of his hiding-place, and with a lighted taper set fire to the feathers. They flared up immediately, and with such a bright light that the soldiers were aroused. The girl ran towards the monarch, wringing her hands and weeping tears of pearl.

"What have you done?" cried she. "How can I now escape my stepmother's vengeance? For it is by her magic that I have been changed into a wild-duck."

When the king had heard all, he ordered some of his soldiers to seize the wife he had married and to take her right out of the country. He sent others to take the wicked stepmother prisoner, and to burn her as a witch. Both commands were instantly carried out. Meanwhile the girl drew from the folds of her gown three small bottles, filled with three different kinds of water, which she had brought from the sea.

The first possessed the virtue of restoring life. This she sprinkled over her brother, whereupon the chill and rigidity of death disappeared, the colour came to his face, and warm

red blood flowed from his wound. Upon the wound she poured water from the second bottle, and it was immediately healed. When she had made use of the third kind of water he opened his eyes, looked at her with astonishment, and threw himself joyfully into her arms.

The king, enraptured at this sight, conducted the two back to the palace.

So instead of a funeral there was a wedding, to which a large number of guests were immediately invited. Thus the orphan maid was married to the king, while her brother became one of his majesty's nobles. And the magnificence of the wedding feast was greater than anything seen or heard of.

THE SLUGGARD

THE SLUGGARD

ON the banks of a certain river, where there was always good fishing, lived an old man and his three sons. The two eldest were sharp-witted, active young men, already married; the youngest was stupid and idle, and a bachelor. When the father was dying, he called his children to him and told them how he had left his property. The house was for his two married sons, with a sum of three hundred florins each. After his death he was buried with great pomp, and after the funeral there was a splendid feast. All these honours were supposed to be for the benefit of the man's soul.

When the elder brothers took possession of their inheritance, they said to the youngest: " Listen, brother; let us take charge of your share of the money, for we intend going out into the world as merchants, and when we have made a great deal of money we will buy you a hat, a sash, and a pair of red boots. You will be better at home; and mind you do as your sisters-in-law tell you."

For a long time this silly fellow had been wanting a cap, a sash, and a pair of red boots, so he was easily persuaded to give up all his money.

The brothers set out on their travels, and crossed the sea in search of fortune. The "fool" of the family remained at home; and, as he was an out-and-out sluggard, he would lie whole days at a time on the warm stove without doing a stroke of work, and only obeying his sisters-in-law with the greatest reluctance. He liked fried onions, potato soup, and cider, better than anything else in the world.

One day his sisters-in-law asked him to fetch them some water.

It was winter, and a hard frost; moreover, the sluggard did not feel at all inclined to go out. So he said, "Go yourselves, I prefer to stay here by the fire."

"Stupid boy, go at once. We will have some onions, potato soup, and cider ready for you when you come back. If you refuse to do what we ask you we shall tell our husbands, and then there will be neither cap, sash, nor red boots for you."

At these words the sluggard thought he had better go. So he rolled off the stove, took a hatchet and a couple of pails, and went down to the river. On the surface of the water, where the ice had been broken, was a large pike. The sluggard seized him by the fins and pulled him out.

"If you will let me go," said the pike, "I promise to give you everything you wish for."

"Well then, I should like all my desires to be fulfilled the moment I utter them."

"You shall have everything you want the moment you pronounce these words :

> 'At my behest, and by the orders of the pike,
>   May such and such things happen, as I like.'"

"Just wait one moment while I try the effect," said the sluggard, and began at once to say :

> "At my behest, and by the orders of the pike,
>   Bring onions, cider, soup, just as I like."

That very moment his favourite dishes were before him. Having eaten a large quantity, he said, "Very good, very good indeed ; but will it always be the same ?"

"Always," replied the pike.

The sluggard put the pike back into the river, and turning towards his buckets, said :

> "At my behest, and by the orders of the pike,
>   Walk home yourselves, my pails—that I should like."

The pails, and the strong rod to which they were fastened, immediately set off and walked solemnly along, the sluggard following them with his hands in his pockets. When they reached the house he put them in their places, and again stretched himself out to enjoy the warmth of the stove. Presently the sisters-in-law said, "Come and chop some wood for us."

"Bother! do it yourselves."

"It is not fit work for women.   Besides, if you don't do it the stove will be cold, and then you will be the chief sufferer. Moreover, pay attention to what we say, for if you do not obey us, there will be no red boots, nor any other pretty things."

The sluggard then just sat up and said :

> "At my behest, and by the orders of the pike,
>   Let what my sisters want be done—that's what I like."

Instantly the hatchet came out from behind a stool and chopped up a large heap of wood, put a part of it on the stove, and retired to its corner.   All this time the sluggard was eating and drinking at his ease.

Another day some wood had to be brought from the forest. Our sluggard now thought he would like to show off before the villagers, so he pulled a sledge out of the shed, loaded it with onions and soup, after which he pronounced the magic words.

The sledge started off, and passing through the village at a rattling pace, ran over several people, and frightened the women and children.

When the forest was reached, our friend looked on while the blocks of wood and faggots cut, tied, and laid themselves on the sledge, after which they set off home again. But when they got to the middle of the village the men, who had been hurt and frightened in the morning, seized hold of the sluggard and pulled him off the sledge, dragging him along by the hair to give him a sound thrashing.

At first he thought it was only a joke, but when the blows hurt his shoulders, he said:

> "At my behest, and by the orders of the pike,
>   Come, faggots, haste, and my assailants strike.'

In a moment all the blocks of wood and faggots jumped off the sledge and began to hit right and left, and they hit so well that the men were glad to get out of the way as best they could.

The sluggard laughed at them till his sides ached; then he remounted his sledge, and was soon lying on the stove again.

From that day he became famous, and his doings were talked about all through the country.

At last even the king heard of him, and, his curiosity being aroused, he sent some of his soldiers to fetch him.

"Now then, booby," said the soldier, "come down off that stove and follow me to the king's palace."

"Why should I? There is as much cider, onions, and soup as I want at home."

The man, indignant at his want of respect, struck him.

Upon which the sluggard said:

> "At my behest, and by the orders of the pike,
>   May this man get a taste of what a broom is like."

A large broom, and not particularly clean, immediately hopped up, and first dipping itself in a pail of water, beat the soldier so mercilessly that he was obliged to escape through the window, whence he returned to the king. His majesty, amazed at the sluggard's refusal, sent another messenger. This man was 'cuter than his comrade, and first made inquiries as to the sluggard's tastes. Then he went up to him and said, "Good-day, my friend; will you come with me to see the king? He wishes to present you with a cap, a waistband, and a pair of red boots."

"With the greatest pleasure; you go on, I will soon overtake you."

Then he ate as much as he could of his favourite dishes and went to sleep on the stove. He slept so long that at last his sisters-in-law woke him up and told him he would be late if he did not at once go to see the king. The lazy fellow said nothing but these words:

> "At my behest, and by the orders of the pike,
>   This stove to carry me before the king I'd like."

At the very same instant the stove moved from its place and carried him right up to the palace door. The king was filled with amazement, and running out, followed by the whole court, asked the sluggard what he would like to have.

"I have merely come to fetch the hat, waistband, and red boots you promised me."

Just then the charming princess Gapiomila came to find out what was going on. Directly the sluggard saw her, he thought her so enchanting that he whispered to himself:

> "At my behest, and by the orders of the pike,
>   That this princess so fair may love me, I should like."

Then he ordered his stove to take him back home, and when there he continued to eat onions and soup and to drink cider.

Meanwhile the princess had fallen in love with him, and begged her father to send for him again. As the sluggard would not consent, the king had him bound when asleep, and thus brought to the palace. Then he summoned a celebrated magician, who at his orders shut the princess and sluggard up in a crystal cask, to which was fastened a balloon well filled with gas, and sent it up in the air among the clouds. The princess wept bitterly, but the fool sat still and said he felt very comfortable. At last she persuaded him to exert his powers, so he said :

> "At my behest, and by the orders of the pike,
>   This cask of crystal earth at once must strike
>   Upon the friendly island I should like."

The crystal cask immediately descended, and opened upon a hospitable island where travellers could have all they wanted by simply wishing for it. The princess and her companion walked about, eating when hungry, and drinking when athirst. The sluggard was very happy and contented, but the lady begged him to wish for a palace. Instantly the palace made its appearance. It was built of white marble, with crystal windows, roof of yellow amber, and golden furniture. She was delighted with it. Next day she wanted a good road made, along which she could go to see her father. Immediately there stretched before them a fairy-like bridge made of crystal, having golden balustrades set with diamonds, and leading right up to the king's palace. The sluggard was just about to accompany the princess when he began to think of his own appearance, and to feel ashamed that such an awkward, stupid fellow as he should walk by the side of such a lovely and graceful creature. So he said :

> " At my behest, and by the orders of the pike,
> To be both handsome, wise, and clever I should like.'

Suddenly he became as handsome, wise, and clever as it was possible to be. Then he got into a gorgeous carriage with Gapiomila, and they drove across the bridge that led to the king's palace.

There they were received with every mark of joy and affection. The king gave them his blessing, and they were married the same evening. An immense number of guests were invited to the wedding feast ; I, too, was there, and drank freely of wine and hydromel. And this is the story I have done my best to tell you as faithfully as possible.

KINKACH MARTINKO

KINKACH MARTINKO

ONCE upon a time there was a poor woman who had an only daughter, named Helen, a very lazy girl. One day when she had refused to do a single thing, her mother took her down to the banks of a stream and began to strike her fingers with a flat stone, just as you do in beating linen to wash it.

The girl cried a good deal. A prince, Lord of the Red Castle, happened at that moment to pass by, and inquired as to the cause of such treatment, for it horrified him that a mother should so ill-use her child.

"Why should I not punish her?" answered the woman.

"The idle girl can do nothing but spin hemp into gold thread."

"Really?" cried he. "Does she really know how to spin gold thread out of hemp? If that be so, sell her to me."

"Willingly; how much will you give me for her?"

"Half a measure of gold."

"Take her," said the mother; and she gave him her daughter as soon as the money was paid.

The prince placed the girl behind him on the saddle, put spurs to his horse, and took her home.

On reaching the Red Castle, the prince led Helen into a room filled from floor to ceiling with hemp, and having supplied her with distaff and spinning-wheel, said, "When you have spun all this hemp into gold thread I will make you my wife."

Then he went out, locking the door after him.

On finding herself a prisoner, the poor girl wept as if her heart would break. Suddenly she saw a very odd-looking little man seated on the window-sill. He wore a red cap, and his boots were made of some strange sort of material.

"Why do you weep so?" he asked.

"I cannot help it," she replied, "I am but a miserable slave. I have been ordered to spin all this hemp into gold thread, but it is impossible, I can never do it, and I know not what will become of me."

"I will do it for you in three days, on condition that at the end of that time you guess my right name, and tell me what the boots I am wearing now are made of."

Without for one moment reflecting as to whether she would be able to guess aright she consented. The uncanny little man burst out laughing, and taking her distaff set to work at once.

All day as the distaff moved the hemp grew visibly less, while the skein of gold thread became larger and larger.

The little man spun all the time, and, without stopping an instant, explained to Helen how to make thread of pure gold. As night drew on he tied up the skein, saying to the girl, "Well, do you know my name yet? Can you tell me what my boots are made of?"

Helen replied that she could not, upon which he grinned and disappeared through the window. She then sat and looked at the sky, and thought, and thought, and thought, and lost herself in conjecturing as to what the little man's name might be, and in trying to guess what was the stuff his boots were made of. Were they of leather? or perhaps plaited rushes? or straw? or cast iron? No, they did not look like anything of that sort. And as to his name—that was a still more difficult problem to solve.

"What shall I call him?" said she to herself—"John? Or Henry? Who knows? perhaps it is Paul or Joseph."

These thoughts so filled her mind that she forgot to eat her dinner. Her meditations were interrupted by cries and groans from outside, where she saw an old man with white hair sitting under the castle wall.

"Miserable old man that I am," cried he: "I die of hunger and thirst, but no one pities my sufferings."

Helen hastened to give him her dinner, and told him to come next day, which he promised to do.

After again thinking for some time what answers she should give the little old man, she fell asleep on the hemp.

The little old man did not fail to make his appearance the first thing next morning, and remained all day spinning the gold thread. The work progressed before their eyes, and it was only when evening came that he repeated his questions. Not receiving a satisfactory answer, he vanished in a fit of mocking laughter. Helen sat down by the window to think; but think as she might, no answer to these puzzling questions occurred to her.

While thus wondering the hungry old man again came by, and she gave him her dinner. She was heart-sick and her eyes were full of tears, for she thought she would never guess the spinner's name, nor of what stuff his boots were made, unless perhaps God would help her.

"Why are you so sad?" asked the old man when he had eaten and drunk; "tell me the cause of your grief, dear lady."

For a long time she would not tell him, thinking it would be useless; but at last, yielding to his entreaties, she gave a full account of the conditions under which the gold thread was made, explaining that unless she could answer the little old man's questions satisfactorily she feared some great misfortune would befall her. The old man listened attentively, then, nodding his head, he said:

"In coming through the forest to-day I passed close to a large pile of burning wood, round which were placed nine iron pots. A little man in a red cap was running round and jumping over them, singing these words:

"My sweet friend, fair Helen, at the Red Castle near,
    Two days and two nights seeks my name to divine.
  She'll never find out, so the third night 'tis clear
    My sweet friend, fair Helen, can't fail to be mine.
  Hurrah! for my name is KINKACH MARTINKO,
  Hurrah! for my boots are of doggies' skin O!"

"Now that is exactly what you want to know, my dear girl; so do not forget, and you are saved."

And with these words the old man vanished.

Helen was greatly astonished, but she took care to fix in her memory all that the good fellow had told her, and then went to sleep, feeling that she could face to-morrow without fear.

On the third day, very early in the morning, the little old man appeared and set busily to work, for he knew that all the hemp must be spun before sunset, and that then he should be able to claim his rights. When evening came all the hemp was gone, and the room shone with the brightness of the golden thread.

As soon as his work was done, the queer little old man with the red cap drew himself up with a great deal of assurance, and with his hands in his pockets strutted up and down before Helen, ordering her to tell him his right name and to say of what stuff the boots were made: but he felt certain that she would not be able to answer aright.

"Your name is KINKACH MARTINKO, and your boots are made of dogskin," she replied without the slightest hesitation.

At these words he spun round on the floor like a bobbin, tore out his hair and beat his breast with rage, roaring so that the very walls trembled.

"It is lucky for you that you have guessed. If you had not, I should have torn you to pieces on this very spot:" so saying he rushed out of the window like a whirlwind.

Helen felt deeply grateful towards the old man who had told her the answers, and hoped to be able to thank him in person. But he never appeared again.

The Prince of the Red Castle was very pleased with her for having accomplished her task so punctually and perfectly, and he married her as he had promised.

Helen was truly thankful to have escaped the dangers that had threatened her, and her happiness as a princess was greater than she had dared hope. She had, too, such a good stock of gold thread that she never had occasion to spin any more all her life long.

THE STORY OF THE PLENTIFUL TABLE-CLOTH, THE AVENGING WAND, THE SASH THAT BECOMES A LAKE, AND THE TERRIBLE HELMET

THE STORY OF THE PLENTIFUL TABLECLOTH, THE AVENGING WAND, THE SASH THAT BECOMES A LAKE, AND THE TERRIBLE HELMET

NOW it once happened that one of the king's herdsmen had three sons. Two of these lads were supposed to be very sharp-witted, while the youngest was thought to be very stupid indeed. The elder sons helped their father to look after the flocks and herds, while the fool, so they called him, was good for nothing but sleeping and amusing himself.

He would pass whole days and nights slumbering peacefully on the stove, only getting off when forced to by others,

or when he was too warm and wished to lie on the other side,
or when, hungry and thirsty, he wanted food and drink.

His father had no love for him, and called him a ne'er-do-
well. His brothers often tormented him by dragging him off
the stove, and taking away his food—indeed, he would many
a time have gone hungry if his mother had not been good to
him and fed him on the quiet. She caressed him fondly, for
why should he suffer, thought she, if he does happen to have
been born a fool? Besides, who can understand the ways of
God? It sometimes happens that the wisest men are not
happy, while the foolish, when harmless and gentle, lead contented lives.

One day, on their return from the fields, the fool's two
brothers dragged him off the stove, and taking him into the
yard, where they gave him a sound thrashing, they turned him
out of the house, saying, "Go, fool, and lose no time, for you
shall have neither food nor lodging until you bring us a
basket of mushrooms from the wood."

The poor lad was so taken by surprise he hardly understood what his brothers wanted him to do. After pondering
for a while he made his way towards a small oak forest, where
everything seemed to have a strange and marvellous appearance, so strange that he did not recognise the place. As he
walked he came to a small dead tree-stump, on the top of
which he placed his cap, saying, "Every tree here raises its
head to the skies and wears a good cap of leaves, but you,
my poor friend, are bare-headed; you will die of cold. You
must be among your brothers, as I am among mine—a born
fool. Take then my cap." And, throwing his arms round
the dead stump, he wept and embraced it tenderly. At that

moment an oak which stood near began to walk towards him as if it were alive. The poor fellow was frightened, and about to run away, but the oak spake like a human being and said, " Do not fly ; stop a moment and listen to me. This withered tree is my son, and up to this time no one has grieved for his dead youth but me. You have now watered him with your tears, and in return for your sympathy you shall henceforward have anything you ask of me, on pronouncing these words :

> " ' O Oak Tree so green, and with acorns of gold,
>   Your friendship to prove I will try ;
>   In Heaven's good name now to beg I'll make bold,
>   My needs, then, oh kindly supply.' "

At the same moment a shower of golden acorns fell. The fool filled his pockets, thanked the oak, and bowing to her returned home.

" Well, stupid, where are the mushrooms ? " cried one of his brothers.

" I have some mushrooms off the oak in my pockets."

" Eat them yourself then, for you will get nothing else, you good-for-nothing. What have you done with your cap ? "

" I put it on a poor stump of a tree that stood by the way-side, for its head was uncovered, and I was afraid it might freeze."

He then scrambled on to the top of the stove, and as he lay down some of the golden acorns fell out of his pocket. So bright were they, they shone like sunbeams in the room. In spite of the fool's entreaties the brothers picked them up and gave them to their father, who hastened to present them to the king, telling him that his idiot son had gathered them in the wood. The king immediately sent a detachment of his guards to the forest to find the oak which bore golden acorns. But their efforts were fruitless, for, though they hunted in every nook and corner of the forest, they found not a single oak that bore acorns of gold.

At first the king was very angry, but when he grew calmer he sent for his herdsman and said to him, "Tell your son, the fool, that he must bring me, by this evening, a cask filled to the brim with these precious golden acorns. If he obeys my commands you shall never lack bread and salt, and you may rest assured that my royal favour will not fail you in time of need."

The herdsman gave his youngest son the king's message.

"The king, I see," he replied, "is fond of a good bargain; he does not ask, he commands—and insists upon a fool fetching him acorns of solid gold in return for promises made of air.   No, I shall not go."

And neither prayers nor threats were of the slightest avail to make him change his mind.   At last his brothers pulled him forcibly off the stove, put his coat on him and a new cap, and dragged him into the yard, where they gave him a good beating and drove him away, saying, " Now, you stupid, lose no time; be off, and be quick.   If you return without the golden acorns you shall have neither supper nor bed."

What was the poor fellow to do?   For a long time he wept, then crossing himself he went in the direction of the forest.   He soon reached the dead stump, upon which his cap still rested, and going up to the mother oak, said to her:

> "O Oak Tree so green, and with acorns of gold,
>   In my helplessness I to thee cry ;
>   In Heaven's great name now to beg I make bold,
>   My pressing needs pray satisfy."

The oak moved, and shook its branches : but instead of golden acorns, a tablecloth fell into the fool's hands.   And the tree said, " Keep this cloth always in your possession, and for your own use.   When you want a benefit by it, you need only say :

> " 'O Tablecloth, who for the poor,
>   The hungry, and thirsty, makes cheer,
>   May he who begs from door to door
>   Feed off you without stint or fear.'"

When it had uttered these words the oak ceased to speak, and the fool, thanking her, bowed, and turned towards home. On his way he wondered to himself how he should tell his brothers, and what they would say, but above all he thought how his good mother would rejoice to see the feast-giving tablecloth. When he had walked about half the distance he met an old beggar who said to him, "See what a sick and ragged old man I am : for the love of God give me a little money or some bread."

The fool spread his tablecloth on the grass, and inviting the beggar to sit down, said :

> "O Tablecloth, who for the poor,
>   The hungry, and thirsty, makes cheer,
> May he who begs from door to door
>   Feed off you without stint or fear."

Then a whistling was heard in the air, and overhead something shone brightly. At the same instant a table, spread as for a royal banquet, appeared before them. Upon it were many different kinds of food, flasks of mead, and glasses of the choicest wine. The plate was of gold and silver.

The fool and the beggar man crossed themselves and began to feast. When they had finished the whistling was again heard, and everything vanished. The fool folded up his tablecloth and went on his way. But the old man said, "If you will give me your tablecloth you shall have this wand in exchange. When you say certain words to it, it will set upon the person or persons pointed out, and give them such a thrashing, that to get rid of it they will give you anything they possess."

The fool thought of his brothers and exchanged the table-cloth for the wand, after which they both went on their respective ways.

Suddenly the fool remembered that the oak had ordered him to keep the tablecloth for his own use, and that by parting with it he had lost the power of giving his mother an agreeable surprise. So he said to the wand :

> " Thou self-propelling, ever willing, fighting Wand,
>   Run quick and bring
>   My feast-providing tablecloth back to my hand,
>   Thy praise I'll sing."

The wand went off like an arrow after the old man, quickly overtook him, and throwing itself upon him began to beat him dreadfully, crying out in a loud voice :

> " For others' goods you seem to have a liking,
>   Stop, thief, or sure your back I'll keep on striking."

The poor beggar tried to run away, but it was of no use, for the wand followed him, striking all the time and repeating the same words over and over again. So in spite of his anxiety to keep the tablecloth he was forced to throw it away and flee.

The wand brought the cloth back to the fool, who again went on his way towards home, thinking of the surprise in store for his mother and brothers. He had not gone very far when a traveller, carrying an empty wallet, accosted him, saying, "For the love of God, give me a small coin or a morsel of food, for my bag is empty and I am very hungry. I have, too, a long journey before me."

The fool again spread his tablecloth on the grass and said :

"O Tablecloth, who for the poor,
  The hungry, and thirsty, makes cheer,
May he who begs from door to door
  Feed off you without stint or fear."

A whistling was heard in the air, something shone brightly overhead, and a table, spread as for a royal feast, placed itself before them. It was laid with a numerous variety of dishes, hydromel and costly wines. The fool and his guest sat down, crossed themselves, and ate to their hearts' content. When they had finished whistling was again heard, and everything vanished. The fool folded the cloth up carefully, and was about to continue his journey when the traveller said, "Will you exchange your tablecloth for my waistband? When you say to it certain words it will turn into a deep lake, upon which you may float at will. The words run thus :

"'O marvellous, wonderful, lake-forming Band,
  For my safety, and not for my fun,
Bear me in a boat on thy waves far from land,
  So that I from my foes need not run."

The fool thought his father would find it very convenient always to have water at hand for the king's flocks, so he gave his tablecloth in exchange for the belt, which he wound round his loins, and taking the wand in his hand, they went off in opposite directions. After a little while the fool began to reflect on what the oak had told him about keeping the table-cloth for his own use, and he remembered, too, that he was depriving himself of the power of giving his mother a pleasant surprise.   Thereupon he said the magic words to his wand:

> "Thou self-propelling, ever willing, fighting Wand,
>   Run quick and bring
>   My feast-providing tablecloth back to my hand,
>   Thy praise I'll sing."

The wand at once started in pursuit of the poor traveller, whom it began to beat, at the same time crying out:

> "For others' goods you seem to have a liking,
>   Stop, thief, or sure your back I'll keep on striking."

The man was scared out of his wits, and tried to escape the wand's blows, but it was of no use, so he was forced to throw the tablecloth away and run at the top of his speed. The wand brought the tablecloth back to his master. The latter hid it under his coat, rearranged the waistband, and taking the faithful wand in his hand, again went towards home. As he walked he rejoiced to think of the pleasure he should have in exercising the wand on his wicked brothers, of his father's satisfaction when, by the help of the waistband, he could always have water for the king's flocks, even in the driest weather, and of his mother's joy on witnessing the wonders of the feast-giving tablecloth. These pleasant thoughts were interrupted by a soldier, lame, clothed in rags, and covered with wounds. He had once been a famous warrior.

"I am pursued by misfortunes," said he to the fool. "I was once a brave soldier, and fought valiantly in my youth. Now I am lamed for life, and on this lonely road have found

no one to give me a morsel of food.   Have pity on me and
give me a little bread."

The fool sat down on the grass, and spreading out his
tablecloth, said :

> "O Tablecloth, who for the poor,
>   The hungry, and thirsty, makes cheer,
> May he who begs from door to door
>   Feed off you without stint or fear."

A whistling was heard in the air, something bright shone
overhead, and then before them stood a table, spread as for
a royal feast, loaded with dainty dishes, mead, and costly
wines.   When they had eaten and drunk as much as they
wanted the whistling was again heard, and then everything
vanished.

The fool was folding up his tablecloth, when the soldier
said :

"Will you give me your tablecloth in exchange for this
six-horned helmet?   It will fire itself off and instantly destroy
the object pointed out.   You have but to turn it round on
your head and repeat these words :

> "'O Magic Helmet, never thou
>   Dost want for powder nor shot ;
> Allay my fears and fire now
>   Just where I point.   Fail not.'

You will see that it fires off immediately : and even if your
enemy were a mile away he would fall."

The fool was delighted with the idea, and thought how
useful such a hat would be in any sudden danger ; it would
even serve him to defend his country, the king, or himself.

So he handed the tablecloth to the soldier, put the helmet on his head, took his wand in his hand, and again set his face towards home.

When he had gone some distance, and the soldier was almost out of sight, he began to think of what the oak had said about not parting with the tablecloth, and of how his dear mother could not now enjoy the pleasant surprise he had been dreaming about. So he said to the wand:

> "Thou self-propelling, ever willing, fighting Wand,
>   Run quick, and bring
>   My feast-providing tablecloth back to my hand,
>   Thy praise I'll sing."

The wand dashed after the soldier, and having reached him began to beat him, crying out:

> "For others' goods you seem to have a liking,
>   Stop, thief, or sure your back I'll keep on striking."

The soldier was still a powerful man, and in spite of his wound turned right about face, intending to give blow for blow. But the wand was too much for him, and he soon found resistance useless. So, overcome by pain rather than fear, he threw away the tablecloth and took to his heels.

The faithful wand brought the tablecloth back to his master, who, glad to have it again, once more turned towards home.

He soon left the forest, crossed the fields, and came in sight of his father's house. At a little distance therefrom his brothers met him, and said crossly, "Well, stupid, where are the golden acorns?"

The fool looked at them and laughed in their faces. Then he said to his wand :

> "O self-propelling, ever willing, fighting Wand
>   Strike with thy usual fire
> My ever-scolding, teasing, worrying brother band,
>   For they have roused my ire."

The wand needed no second bidding, and darting out of his hand began to thrash the brothers soundly, crying out like a reasoning creature :

> "Your brother has often your blows felt, alack !
> Now taste it yourselves ; hope you like it, whack, whack."

The brothers were overpowered, and felt all the while as if boiling water were being poured over their heads. Yelling with pain they began to run at full speed, and soon disappeared with clouds of dust flying round them.

The wand then came back to the fool's hand. He went into the house, climbed on the stove, and told his mother all that had happened. Then he cried :

> "O Tablecloth, who for the poor,
>   The hungry, and thirsty, makes cheer,
> Let us within our cottage door
>   Feed off you without stint or fear."

A whistling was heard in the air, something bright shone overhead, and then a table, laid as for a royal banquet, was placed before them, covered with dainty meats, glasses, and bottles of mead and wine. The whole service was of gold and silver. As the fool and his mother were about to begin the feast the herdsman entered. He stopped, dumb with amazement, but when invited to partake, began to eat and drink with great enjoyment.

At the end of the meal the whistling was again heard, and everything vanished completely.

The herdsman set off in hot haste to the court, to tell the king of this new marvel. Thereupon his majesty sent one of his heroes in search of the fool, whom he found stretched on the stove.

"If you value your life, listen, and obey the king's orders," said the paladin. "He commands you to send him by me your tablecloth, then you shall have your share of his royal favour. But if not you will always remain a poor fool, and will, moreover, be treated as a refractory prisoner. We teach them how to behave ; you understand?"

"Oh yes, I understand." And then he pronounced the magic words :

> "O self-propelling, ever willing, fighting Wand,
>   Go, soundly thrash that man—
> The most deceiving, dangerous wretch in all the land,
>   So hurt him all you can."

The wand sprang from the fool's hand with the speed of lightning and struck the paladin three times in the face. He immediately fled, but the wand was after him, hitting him all the time, and crying out :

> " Mere promises are children's play,
> So do not throw your breath away,
> But think of something true to say,
> You rogue, when next you come our way."

Defeated and filled with consternation, the paladin returned to the king and told him about the wand, and how badly he had been beaten. When the king heard that the fool possessed a wand that struck of itself, he wanted it so much that for a time he forgot all about the tablecloth, and sent some of his soldiers with orders to bring him back the wand.

When they entered the cottage, the fool, as usual, was lying on the stove.

" Deliver up the wand to us instantly," said they ; " the king is willing to pay any price you ask, but if you refuse he will take it from you by force."

Instead of replying the fool unwound the waistband, saying to it as he did so :

> " O marvellous, wonderful, lake-forming Band,
>> For my safety, and not for my fun,
>> Bear me in a boat on thy waves far from land,
>> So that I from my foes need not run."

There was a shimmering in the air, while at the same moment everything around them disappeared, and a beautiful lake, long, wide, and deep, was seen, surrounded by green fields. Fish with golden scales and eyes of pearls played in the clear water. In the centre, in a small silver skiff, rowed a man, whom the soldiers recognised as the fool.

They remained some time looking at this miracle, and then ran off to tell the king. Now when the king heard thereof he was so anxious to possess the lake, or rather the waistband that produced the lake, that he sent a whole battalion of soldiers to take the fool prisoner.

This time they managed to get hold of him while he was

asleep, but as they were about to tie his hands he turned his
hat round and said :

> " O Magic Helmet, never thou
>   Dost want for powder nor shot,
>   Allay my fears and fire now
>   Just where I point.   Fail not."

Instantly a hundred bullets whistled through the air, amid
clouds of smoke and loud reports.   Many of the soldiers fell
dead, others took refuge in the wood, whence they returned
to the king to give an account of what had taken place.

Whereupon the king flew into a violent rage, furious that
he had as yet failed to take the fool.   But his wish to possess
the feast-giving tablecloth, the magic wand, the lake-forming
sash, and above all the helmet with twenty-four horns, was
stronger than ever.

Having reflected for some days on the best ways and
means to attain his object, he resolved to try the effect of
kindness, and sent for the fool's mother.

"Tell your son, the fool," said his majesty to the woman,
"that my charming daughter and I send greeting, and that we
shall consider it an honour if he will come here and show us
the marvellous things he possesses.   Should he feel inclined
to make me a present of them, I will give him half my kingdom
and will make him my heir.   You may also say that the
princess, my daughter, will choose him for her husband."

The good woman hastened home to her son, whom she
advised to accept the king's invitation and show him his
treasures.   The fool wound the waistband round his loins,
put the helmet on his head, hid the tablecloth in his breast,

took his magic wand in his hand, and started off to go to the court.

The king was not there on his arrival, but he was received by the paladin, who saluted him courteously. Music played, and the troops did him military honours—in fact, he was treated far better than he had expected. On being presented to the king he took off his helmet, and bowing low, said: "O king, I am come to lay at the foot of your throne my table-cloth, waistband, wand, and helmet. In return for these gifts I beg that your favour may be shown to the most humble of your subjects."

"Tell me then, fool, what price you want for these goods?"

"Not money, sire, a fool of my sort cares very little about money. Has not the king promised my mother that he will give me in exchange the half of his kingdom, and the hand of his daughter in marriage? These are the gifts I claim."

After these words the paladin was filled with envy at the good fortune of the fool, and made a sign for the guards to enter. The soldiers seized the poor fellow, dragged him out into the courtyard, and they killed him treacherously to the sound of drums and trumpets, after which they covered him over with earth.

Now it happened that when the soldiers stabbed him his blood spurted out, and some of the drops fell beneath the princess's window. The maiden wept bitterly at the sight, watering the blood-stained ground with her tears. And lo! marvellous to relate, an apple-tree grew out of the blood-sprinkled earth. And it grew so rapidly that its branches soon touched the windows of her rooms; by noon it was covered with blossom, while at eventide ripe red apples hung thereon. As the princess was admiring them she noticed that one of the apples trembled, and when she touched it, it fell into the bosom of her dress. This took her fancy, and she held it in her hand.

Meanwhile the sun had set, night had fallen, and every one in the palace was asleep, except the guard, the paladin, and the princess. The guard, sword in hand, patrolled up and down, for it was his duty. The princess toyed with her pretty little apple, and could not sleep. The paladin, who had gone to bed, was aroused by a sound that made his blood run cold, for the avenging wand stood before him and began to beat him soundly. And although he rushed from the room trying to escape from it, it followed him, crying out :

> " False paladin, you worthless man,
>   Do not so envious be ;
>   Why act unjustly, when you can
>   Both just and honest be ?
>   For others' goods why have you such a liking ?
>   You rogue, you thief, be sure I'll keep on striking."

The unhappy man wept and cried for mercy, but the wand still continued to strike.

The princess was distressed on hearing these cries of distress, and she watered her much-cherished apple with her tears. And, strange to tell, the apple grew and changed its shape. Thus continuing to change, it suddenly turned into a handsome young man, even the very same who had been killed that morning.

" Lovely princess, I salute you," said the fool. " The cunning of the paladin caused my death, but with your tears you have restored me to life. Your father promised to give you to me : are you willing?"

"If such be the king's wish, I consent," replied she, as she gave him her hand with a tender look.

As he spoke the door opened, admitting the helmet, which placed itself upon his head; the sash, which wound itself round his waist; the tablecloth, which hid itself in one of his pockets; and the avenging wand, which placed itself in his hand. Then came the king, all out of breath, and wondering what the noise was about. He was amazed to see the fool alive again, and even more so that he should be with the princess.

The young fellow, fearing the king's wrath, cried out :

"O marvellous, wonderful, lake-forming Band,
    For my safety, and not for my fun,
    Bear us in a boat on thy waves far from land,
    So that we from our foes need not run."

There was a shimmering in the air, and then everything disappeared, while on the lawn before the palace stretched a wide deep lake, in the crystal water of which swam little fish with eyes of pearl and scales of gold. Far away rowed the princess and the fool in a silver skiff. The king stood on the shores of the lake and signed to them to return. When they had landed they knelt at his feet and avowed their mutual love. Upon which his majesty bestowed his blessing, the lake disappeared, and they again found themselves in the princess's apartments.

The king called a special meeting of his council, at which he explained how things had turned out—that he had made the fool his heir, and betrothed him to his daughter, and had put the paladin in prison.

The fool gave the king his magic treasures, and told him what words to say in each case.

Next day all their wishes were fulfilled. The fool of the family was married to the princess, and at the same time received half the kingdom, with the promise of succession to the throne. And the wedding feast, to which all the rich and noble of the land were invited, exceeded in its magnificence and splendour any other festival ever seen or heard of.

THE END